ANDROMEDA

Ginny Lynn

Dearest hug *Ginny Lynn*

Mainstream Romance

Wench Writer

Secret Cravings Publishing
www.secretcravingspublishing.com

A Secret Cravings Publishing Book
Mainstream Romance

Andromeda
Copyright © 2013 Ginny Lynn
Print ISBN: 978-1-61885-772-9

First E-book Publication: March 2013
First Print Publication: July 2013

Cover design by Dawné Dominique
Edited by Megan Koenen
Proofread by Renee Waring
All cover art and logo copyright © 2013 by Secret Cravings
Publishing

PUBLISHER
Secret Cravings Publishing
www.secretcravingspublishing.com

DEDICATION

To those who lovingly pushed me from the nest, to watch me take flight.

ANDROMEDA

Ginny Lynn
Copyright © 2013

Chapter One

Cartagena de Indias 1551

I snatched up the dagger that my father kept hidden and peeked over the cluttered countertop. Perseus raced from the kitchen and slashed the squat bald pirate across the face before he knocked Perseus unconscious with his sword hilt. Quickly after, my sisters and mother were all thrown to the floor, joining the now still body of my twin brother. A wet darkness pooled near them from Perseus' head. My little sister, Cassiopeia, cringed from the puddle as she gathered her full skirt, weeping.

The pirate with the bleeding face ripped the apron off my mother and held it to his sliced cheek. The wound would scar the entire side of the fiend's face. "We wants all the shillin' 'n any silver ye got."

"You can have it, if you will just leave us be," answered my mother.

In the face of this, my mother remained a protective force over her children. Boisterous laughter rang through the room. Her chin remained up, not flinching from their amusement at our expense.

A tall lean man with loosely curled golden hair strolled into the bar and spotted me as I watched from my hidden place behind the shelf. How had he known I'd been hiding here? I'd been a statue as I had waited to strike at the opportune moment. What had given me away?

"Ye be in no position to negotiate," he finally spoke.

Though he was a ways away from me, I bravely pointed the dagger in the direction of his heart. "I disagree."

I stood tall as he came closer to me, stopping in front of the dagger and letting it push slowly through the fabric of his tunic. His intense black eyes held my frightened ones, daring me to act. But even as I tried to dig the dagger into his chest with more force, it would not pierce his skin. Something, some unknown force, held me in position. I could think of tearing the sharp edge through his rib, but my body would not obey me. What magic was this? "You have power and courage, my young beauty." He inhaled deeply, seeming to taste the air around me. "Yes, much power, a very rare find. I could use someone like you in my voyages."

"I am not inclined to accept such an offer. Please take what silver and coin we have and leave us in peace."

He simply laughed at my plea and it rolled across my skin in a shudder. "Silly child. I am a man who takes what he wants, which includes ye. Ye think that ye can just send me on my way? I find ye more and more intriguing with each passing moment. Courage and fire smolders beneath that skin. I must have ye now. And with me, the world will be open to ye. Ye can use your power to see me to the future while your body warms my bed at night."

He reached down toward me and skimmed his hand down my tense face. I spat at his feet, unable to move from him. Silence owned the room as we waited to see if he would strike me for my arrogance

"Wench! Ye meager life is to be changed forever, so regard me with more respect."

I cursed him in my grandmother's gypsy tongue as I fought with my body to move away from this fiend. He shook his handsome head and smiled a chilling smile that made my heart skip a beat. Those magnetic coal black eyes focused on mine and I became so enthralled that I was unable to register any other person in the room but him. It was if a silk veil had been placed to hide away the chaos around us. In this new sight, he was magnificent, a golden rogue.

"Do you want to live?"

"Yes."

"What is your name, *belle*?" His voice held a hint of France.

"Andromeda Ortiz."

"Ah, Andromeda. A fitting name for someone who could hold the very world in her small hands."

He snatched the dagger from my shaking hands with little effort and placed it firmly on the counter beside the dirty ale mugs. As he dragged me against his surprisingly hard chest, all conviction to fight left me, and I became a puppet to his will.

He whispered, "I have been remiss in my duties. Let me introduce myself. I am Captain Damien Anastase and you, Andromeda, will be mine for all eternity."

"I will pledge myself to your service, if you swear to let my family go."

The spell he'd placed on me cracked into pieces as I heard my brother's plea for our safety. Blood shimmered on his injured scalp as he leaned his battered body against the scarred wood banister. But at least he was still alive. My would-be captor turned around to face him.

"Ah, such a gallant young man. What do you offer me for their freedom?"

"No, Perseus, don't promise him anything," I said.

But Perseus would not be swayed. "Father entrusted me to protect you, so I must do this," Perseus said to me. Then to my blonde captor, "I am willing to sail on your ship, even become first mate, if you will take our coin and leave this place behind."

My captor thought on it a moment, seemingly unaware of me as I again and again tried and failed to yank myself from his vile clutches. "That is a fair trade," he said, finally letting me go. "Jean Luc, take him to the ship." The slashed face pirate made a move towards us.

"Aye, Captain."

"My family, sir? I cannot depart without knowing they will remain unharmed. What assurance can you give me?" Perseus' voice rang clear and unafraid.

"They will be taken care of, just as ye will. Now leave before I dispense with the good fortune that I have granted ye."

Perseus looked at me. "I do this for the good of my family and nothing more."

His dedication to us would have him indebted for the remainder of his life. The barbaric nature of this would tear my family apart and I would never see him again.

Before those thoughts could form words in my mouth, Jean Luc snatched Perseus out the door. And then I heard his cry.

"Perseus?" I yelled and tried to run to him, but was captured by the captain.

I tried to wiggle away, but his voice made me stop completely. "Look at me, Andromeda."

As I turned my head and stared into those ominous dark eyes, my mind was blank once again. I barely felt him palm my right cheek and lean my head to the side so my throat was exposed. I think I whimpered. He lowered his lips and pain stabbed through my neck. It was then that everything came rushing back into sharp focus. I cried out and thrashed against him, but to no avail. He was a solid wall that I could not tear down. I felt the violating draw of those lips against my trembling flesh. A wave of weakness rode through my body as his mouth sucked at my aching neck.

My body leaned into his frame, the simple movement feeling foreign to me. No one, let alone a man, had ever embraced me in such an intimate way. Through all the other emotions whipping through my body, it was a wave of anger that presented itself most clearly. I had only shared one chaste stolen kiss as a young maiden, and this heathen had taken more liberties in the short time since he barged into my house, than any suitor had been allowed. How dare he? As that thought left me, so too did every ounce of energy from my body. My will to make this fiend unhand me was taken away from me, no matter how desperate I felt. I swooned, and the room and its contents faded into oblivion as this strange kiss took the last of my consciousness.

* * * *

I woke to a nightmare that rocked and heaved with the smell of the sea heavy in the air. I couldn't open my heavy eyelids, but I registered a male voice above me as I lay on my back. The sound of it was familiar, but not one of the voices of the men in my family.

"Ye must drink, my Andromeda. Drink and come back to me as a lover. Ye be the path to gain us riches beyond our wildest dreams. Drink and become eternal. Drink and join me."

I smelled copper and salt under my nose and a thirst like none other seized me. My throat burned as if hell itself had taken it by force. I had to have *it* to quench this awful feeling. I must. I opened my mouth as something firm pressed against it. *It* filled my mouth, and I moaned from the rich taste.

"Feed, my dear. Feed and wake to a new world."

I did feed and I became an animal as I took *it* into my mouth. I moaned as it slid down my parched throat. I savored it. I drank it in. Warmth spread through my body that had just been so incredibly cold, running through my veins like fire, burning my slow beating heart. I had no knowledge of what *it* was, but I knew I would die without it. It snatched me back to life. It was the water that fed me in the cruelest desert.

Too soon, he took that liquid away. An ache deep in my muscles made me cry out for release, for more. Wrenching spasms shook me as my body revolted against me. The pain grew so vast and I lost myself in a fire that left me as ash. I gladly faded into oblivion again.

* * * *

I felt weightless, and then a rushing pressure as I heard a roar in my ears. This sensation was soothing after the intense heat of the fire that had burned my tortured soul. I sank into the cool comfort that embraced me as I became one with its small relief. As I slept, something large and strong nudged me. I opened my heavy eyes to see that I was deep underwater. Then I panicked. How could I possibly be alive in the ocean? I then realized I wasn't breathing. Why wasn't I breathing? I forced myself to take in air, knowing it was seawater as it filled my chest. But I wasn't drowning. Had I already died? My limbs were entangled in the sharp edges of a coral reef, and blood welled in the water as I tried to free myself. I calmed myself when I saw that Perseus was in the coral next to me, awake and struggling as well. He quickly broke free. It was then I saw that sharks had smelled the blood from our injuries and had begun to circle us.

Perseus made eye contact with me as the sharks circled closer and closer. He nodded up and I knew he wanted us to swim to the surface. We had nearly made it before two of the sharks made their move. Perseus went under just before I did, and we fought to have our limbs released from the teeth that had us trapped. The shark that had me shook my body violently but was unable to rip my limbs apart. I knew Perseus was the same. I struck out and kicked myself free, causing the shark to bleed from the force behind my movements. The smell of the sharks was a similar smell to the one I had drunk from earlier, but not nearly as intoxicating.

My mind took over any rational thought as I went after the shark's blood like it had gone after mine. Perseus took heed and we drank heavily before swimming to the debris-covered sand of our island shore.

Smoke billowed along the coastline. The few boats that were there had no one on board. There wasn't a living soul on the worn dock. There was only the silence of the sea as it beat against the sand.

Since our youth, our grandmother had told us legends of the undead that fed on the lives of the mortals around them. They feasted on whole villages and used superior strength to take their prey. Some had been devious men who had used mind tricks to amass great wealth. We knew what we had become. But we vowed not to be the same as the monsters in her tales or like the monster who had changed our lives. We would continue on as we had been, protecting each other from all of the evils that came our way as we used our new skills.

No sounds arose as we made the trip back to the tavern. We salvaged what we could from the ruins of our home and buried the bodies that were once our generous neighbors. Even the fishmonger had been filleted, thrown on his bloody back as food for the birds and crabs. This man had helped to put food on our meager tables but now he was an empty shell. There would be no more comfort for this place; it had been turned into a place of nightmares and curses.

As we found the bodies of our family, we realized the captain had not kept his word and had tortured them all to death, each in a distinct way. Even if he had not been the one to shove a rusty blade into my mother's gut, he had brought this upon us all. My brother and I buried the mangled and dismembered bodies of our family in the small garden that stood outside the tavern's back door. The small gypsy ceremony we held there gave us no peace as we faced the ghosts of our cherished family and friends.

We wondered how we had been selected to survive, even if in this damned state. We knew then that we had to find a new home, create new lives, and come to terms with what we had become. We would have an eternity to mourn this day.

* * * *

October 2009

It was just before six pm and time to get ready for work. I slid out of my luxuriant sheets, and in fifteen minutes I had showered, dressed, and run mousse through my long black ringlets. Makeup was minimal enough that only eyeliner and pale rose lip-gloss were needed. I stepped into my comfortable flats, grabbed my bangle bracelets and hobo bag, and made my way to the darkening street.

It was only a couple of miles to work, so I normally walked there, even in the pouring rain. My vintage Jaguar convertible was only for further away trips, and thus was only needed a few times a month. Being so close to River Street in Savannah put me near everything except a large department store and a grocery store. Although I hardly ever ate, so a grocery store wasn't necessary.

I inhaled the scents around me as I walked along the cooling sidewalks. I gathered the scents of sin, blood, and fear from several miles away as I became aware of my surroundings. The blood hardly affected me; I'd long since gotten over the hunger that came with such a curse.

The use of my heightened senses was how I chose my prey; I hunted only the vile people who lived off hurting others. It was surprisingly easy for me to find prey, and once I did I could usually lure them in with just a simple look. I tried to never regret what I was or what I did to survive. Daily, I reminded myself that I did good deeds just as well as evil, and did my part for the betterment of the world. For lesser evils I encountered, I could compel someone to stop drinking or stop beating their wife with a simple thought placed into their muddled minds. My brother tried to be like me in this aspect, but he lived with regret, and it was a bag that weighed down his strong shoulders. If seeing our slaughtered family wasn't enough, it'd been compounded when he hadn't been able to stop his one true love from dying an excruciating death.

It had taken many years for him to get over that, and he had vowed that he would never change a person or attack an innocent soul. I hadn't seen him show any interest in having a solid relationship since then. He said he was happy with just his businesses and me.

I caught an exotic scent in the air and knew it was my best friend and co-worker, Danya. I could hear her running to the door just around the corner from me. She hated to be late just as much as I did, and the human pace that I was forced to walk in order to blend in made me laugh. A human could blink and never see me go from one block to the other. As old as I was, I could do lots of other interesting things, but living as a human meant I had to behave as one, at least as much as possible. Besides, I appreciated simple things like walking slow and having a best friend.

"Slow down, Danya. You still have ten minutes before you start your shift," I said as I came around the corner behind her.

She grimaced at me. "I just added a new alarm to my grocery list. Mine died of natural causes last night."

I bet it really died from abuse, but I wasn't about to say that out loud. I unlocked the door for her as she shouldered through the doorway with her bag and coffee in hand. Most people thought it was unusual to be drinking fully leaded coffee at six p.m. but we worked from six-thirty p.m. to three a.m. and then went home to do things around our houses. She and I worked the same nights, which had been the catalyst to us becoming best friends.

Danya was a woman who stood five-feet-seven with dirty blonde hair and hazel eyes. I could never understand how a woman who was Indian, Spanish, Russian, and Irish could have that coloring, but when I asked she always remarked that she was the best of the mutts and left it at that. She also spoke six different languages and knew how to curse in all of them, and wasn't afraid to do so.

If the day ever came for her to find out our true identities, I'd hate to compel her. But I'd do that if it meant her not turning out like Valentina, my brother's deceased fiancé. I just hoped that if she did find out she'd stay the same considerate person as she was now or at least be intrigued, like Bambara. That simple thought brought on a psychic vision.

I was receiving an image for tomorrow, as I saw an invoice for a towing service. They weren't always this clear, but this one was certain. The car wasn't filled in yet, just the date and address.

"Hey Danya, that appointment you have tomorrow?" I said.

"What did you see?" This type of conversation happened so frequently Danya was hardly surprised by my unprompted question.

"Don't go down Drayton towards East Harris. They're roofing and you'll get a flat tire."

"Well, okay. Thanks hun."

"You're welcome. And get the tomato red polish this time."

"Oh, why's that?"

"Because it looks good on you, silly." I ducked as I saw the rag being flung at me before she even threw it in the air. It landed softly on the table beside me and she laughed.

"Why do I have to be best friends with a psychic?" She grumbled with a smile. I laughed right back at her, this routine a familiar one.

By eight-thirty, people had lined up to have their fortunes read. I'd gotten so comfortable with reading fortunes through the years that it barely took any power to do it these days. In the old days, I was tired after one lesson with my grandmother. Now I could read twenty-five people without even needing a break.

Another hour later, I had a vision of Perseus as he headed home in his convertible Porsche. He kept his focus on his businesses and me, in that order, and he was happy that he'd found a property that could be used to open another bar. The one I worked at was named Mythology, but his next venture would be named Medusa's Manor. This next one would be jazz based and located in Louisiana. Once I came out of the vision, I noticed Danya hadn't taken a break yet so I nudged her hip.

"Hey, let me take the next few so you can take a break."

She nodded and stepped aside for me before she headed into the kitchen were she kept a stash of healthy snacks for herself. I tended bar for about five minutes before she came back with tortilla chips in a coffee filter. I snagged one and then handed over the beer that I'd poured for my customer.

Yes, I can eat as well as drink. I found many years ago that there were ancient herbs I could use to process anything in my stomach. I got the herbs two to three times a year from my cherished cohort, Bambara, in Louisiana. She was a third generation voodoo priestess I had known all of her life.

I'd been a friend to the women in her family for two hundred years, each one of them taking care of Perseus and I like we were blood relatives. Bambara admired our pledge to only feed from evil people and thought it was humorous that we did so much to hide what we were. She made no bones about being a powerful woman, and people knew to respect her, even if they didn't like her. She had been very useful over the years in helping with our masquerade as humans.

She knew that mirrors would not show our reflection so she had made mirrors lined with real silver and liquefied herbs that actually reflected our appearances. I had several in my house and Perseus had them installed in every business he owned. She had wanted to help us with the fact that regular cameras couldn't capture our image but then digital ones came out, and the problem solved itself.

"Hey, Perseus should be here any minute now. I spoke to him on break and he's excited about the new location," I said.

"It'll be good to see Percy again."

My co-worker had been crushing on my brother since the first time they'd met, but to her credit, she was smart enough to act professional about her boss. Even if I hadn't been psychic, I could tell how she felt about him.

"He asked if I wanted to come check it out before he signed the papers and I think I will."

A few moments later, Perseus walked through the front door with a smile for Danya and me. Her face held a radiant smile before she ducked her head back down toward her register. His expression changed when he caught the look on Danya's face and I wondered if Perseus would ever take her up on these hints. I hated that he felt the need to push women away but he had a valid reason for not wanting to be involved, so I couldn't blame him. He was the poster child for the strong silent type.

I went back to my table to tell fortunes for the rest of the night and we both left Perseus to his paperwork. A short while later a new vision hit, and I clutched the chair in fear. I saw Danya, bloody and in agony, like Valentina had been, so long ago. Perseus held her hand as she fought for her life. My mind screamed as I snapped out of the vision, but I stopped and assessed what I'd seen before making any conclusions. I must've looked stricken because the lady at my table asked if I was okay. I told her that I'd received a vision for a friend and finished her fortune before I excused myself.

I all but ran into Perseus' office and put my hands against the sides of his face. He knew it was a vision and braced himself as he gathered the images that I'd seen. He stopped, his mind kept saying "No" over and over again, like he did in my vision. When it was over, I dropped onto his desk and stared into space. It took a couple of minutes for the dread to leave my body.

"She was at the water line but I can't get a time line or see anything else that would help us."

"I could only see the blood," Perseus whispered.

I need more in order to stop it, so I closed my eyes and concentrated.

"I can't see where the blood came from, but her ribs were broken."

"Something blocked us from seeing the details, or facts haven't been determined as of yet." I slid off the desktop.

"It happens at night so I'll keep an eye on her every night until this clears up," he said as he hugged me.

"We can't tempt fate by telling her what I've seen. It'd be too much to tell my best friend that I've seen her covered in her own blood. I can't even see if she ends up okay."

"Stop, Andy." He used my nickname while his emotions rode high. "You'll make it worse by worrying. So just relax and we'll keep her safe. We have to."

I wasn't sure if it was the pain of potentially losing her, or the fact that he couldn't lose anyone else like that, but we'd use our powers to keep her safe, one way or the other.

Chapter Two

It was last call at the bar, so I shook off the visions as best I could and went outside his office to help clean up. The disbursing crowd and being close to Danya made the grimness fade, and by closing time I'd gotten better. When we left Mythology, Perseus snuck out the back to watch over Danya as she walked to her car. I used the alone time to try and pinpoint a timeline for the injury to Danya but only ended up with a headache.

I was pouring a drink in the parlor by the time Perseus came in. Danya had gotten home without incident and Perseus had run through her house and slipped out before she'd even driven a mile. I got out a second glass as he grabbed my full one. I took a teaspoon of the special herbs Bambara gave me for my digestion and washed it down with some vodka I'd poured. It had been a couple of days and I knew I needed to feed soon, so after walking home with Perseus, I headed upstairs to change into jeans and a worn t-shirt to hunt in. Perseus decided to come with me and held my hand as we headed to the front porch. We quickly picked up an evil presence two miles away and we ran those two miles faster than humans could walk two blocks.

The prey was a drug dealer who was trying to subdue one of his young female clients with the intent to rape her. We wouldn't allow that. Perseus jumped the man as I sucked the vile drugs from her dilated veins. Perseus instilled fear into the drug dealer while I showed the seventeen year old a vision of her mother who cried over a small coffin as it lowered into the cold, still earth. We left the unconscious man in the dumpster and left the woman on the swing in her backyard, then went home.

I couldn't shake the tension that tightened my psychic thread from the events of the day, but I forced myself to ignore it and lay my head on pillows that contained bagged soil from my homeland inserted inside the fluffy layers. It was a myth that vampires slept in coffins, but we did need the soil to maintain our powers plus ensure restful sleep. Perseus had identical bags and always carried one with him when he traveled. We never had a peaceful sleep without them being present and we didn't want to know how long we could go without. Even the dead had to sleep sometime.

In my dream, I caught a glimpse of black eyes just as my alarm jolted me awake from a less than peaceful sleep. With my head in a fog, I stumbled through my morning routine, finishing by making some strong coffee. I took a sip and realized I was worse than I thought if I was forgetting to add my herbs to the steaming mug.

This thought was re-enforced as I uncharacteristically walked right into someone tall and solid on my way to work. He grabbed my hand and my sudden stop made my coffee slosh over the rim and singe my fingers. It stung for only a second before I healed up.

"You okay?" A husky voice asked me.

"Yes, I'm fine. Sorry about that. I'm usually a lot more observant, but I didn't sleep well last night. I mean, this morning."

I finally looked up and saw a smile on the face of a gorgeous man with shoulder length sandy blonde hair. He had a camera in his hand and a tripod set up between his long legs. Apparently he had been taking shots of the buildings when I had run into the back of him. I noticed it was not digital and backed up a step.

"I hope I didn't hurt your camera." I bit my lip.

"No, it's fine."

I noticed the cap was still on and the tension fell from my shoulders.

"I understand sleeping issues very well. I have a rare form of narcolepsy." He gave me a smile that lit up his chocolate brown eyes.

"Well, I'll let you get back to your work. Sorry again for not paying attention." I walked past him with a wave over my shoulder.

"Just make sure you don't walk in front of any traffic," he laughed.

I laughed back after realizing I'd be the only thing that walked away if that happened.

I snapped out of my fog and smiled at that mental image as Danya walked up the sidewalk. "Thanks for that tip yesterday. A woman with a flat tire walked into the salon and needed a tow truck. That could've easily been me."

We walked in, put our stuff down, and she looked at me again.

"Wait a minute, is that coffee? And were you just smiling? Give."

I told her about the guy I ran into.

"Was he cute?"

"Yes, he was good looking." Why lie?

"Well, knowing you, you didn't even get his name. I would've been all over that, and that fact alone shows how different we are."

"You have no idea how different we truly are, Danya."

One day we'd sit down and she'd ask me what I'd been dreading for quite some time. But until then I was happy to keep her in ignorant bliss.

"Okay and if you have something to say, then just pull me to the side and ask, anytime." She hugged me just as Perseus walked in.

"Hello ladies, can I get in on that?" He squeezed us into a big bear hug, and we all laughed loudly.

We'd had a good night working the crowd at the bar, and were worn out when we all went home to our separate beds. Danya was watched over by her unknown security guard, Perseus, and I was still awake long after Perseus had fallen asleep and the sun had come up. I lay in bed and listened to sounds outside my double balcony doors. I heard a whisper and the tone made me straighten up in bed. I listened for it again but still couldn't quite place it. I then tuned out everything but the voice and had to wait several minutes before I heard it again. Then I heard it crystal clear. The voice was male and said my name softly. I couldn't tell if it was actually spoken or someone was trying to find me mentally. I felt a jolt when it came again and a sharp ache settled into the top of my head. I held my head and tried to locate the voice, but received only more pain instead.

Perseus shot into my room and grabbed me as my fingers clinched in my hair. I felt crowded when he entered my thoughts to repel the pain away. My eyes shot open as I heard a deep laugh. I screamed as my mind reeled from the pressure it caused in my skull. Then it was gone.

I had been mentally shoved from the connection. I focused my eyes and saw Perseus leaning over me. I let go of the sheets and

wrapped my arms around his cold body. It took a while for the
feeling to come back in my numb limbs.

When it had faded, I looked into Perseus' eyes. "What
happened?"

"You were in so much pain. I had to stop it."

"What did you see?"

"I saw a man's form and he laughed knowing you were in
pain. I went in to stop him and absorbed as much as I could, but
you felt it anyway." He rocked me in his arms as he had when we
were very young, and I welcomed it.

"Can you tell who it is? Has this ever happened to you?"

"I can't tell you anything else. I'm sorry. Just catch your
breath and shove the negativity away. I know that's easier said
than done, but you'll be in worse shape if you reach for that
connection again. Trust me." He kissed the top of my head.

I nodded into his chest and sat for a few minutes as he
continued to rock me. As the sun faded away, I moved away from
him, stood up, and headed toward my closet. He wanted me to
shake it off, and I'd do as he had instructed. I cleared my mind of
the whole thing and immediately felt better. I grabbed some worn
jeans and a long sleeved t-shirt from my closet.

"Perseus, I want to drive down to Wassaw National Wildlife
Refuge and check out the dunes. You know we had fun doing that
as children. Say you'll come with me?"

"I have something I have to do, but I can feed with you when
you come back. Is that okay?" He stood by my bedroom door and
looked at the floor.

I was disappointed, but tried not to show it. "Yes, that'd be
fine. Let me know if you change your mind." He left before I
finished my shower.

Needing to get gas before the long drive, I got out my Jaguar
from the garage and headed down the back alley toward the gas
station. I felt a presence while I pumped gas but a quick look about
showed no one was around. I had to release some of the tension I'd
been feeling so much of lately, so I took the top down, tied a scarf
over my mane and headed toward the coast. I always felt free when
I had the wind on my skin, whether it was from running or driving.
I'd bought a convertible just for that reason and enjoyed every
minute of driving it. I could sense any cop or wreck in my path

miles before I could reach them. I knew where more humans frequented so I avoided those streets.

An hour later and I pulled my car into a place that was safe from park employees. I tossed my sandals onto the soft leather seat; having feet like mine, vampire feet, meant I had no real need for shoes. Brambles and jagged rocks never affected me. I ran as far as I could up and down the property line and only stopped when Perseus mentally checked in on me a few hours later. He faded away when he was assured that I was okay.

After a few hours of running through the refuge, I decided to start back toward home. I found Perseus on the porch swing, so I pulled the car around back, parked it, and ran to meet up with him. I held out my hand and asked him where we were headed. He said he'd heard about a rapist in Poole and wanted to find him. I was game and off we ran. No one saw us as we ran through the dark streets, and into Poole. It was like we had wings. *If only.*

As usual, we were quick to catch his scent of fear and lust. It was scary how I could enjoy the hunt so much, but I always did. Maybe because this was the only time we allowed ourselves to be the true monsters of legends. Or at least the type of monsters that took out the bad people in the world instead of the other way around.

When we left the rapist in the police parking lot, we held hands and ran home. I immediately went for another hot bath; I always felt dirty after feeding. I lit my incense as I bathed away the man's sins.

I dragged the washcloth over myself and felt a presence but I ignored it. I'd gone from my toes to my thighs when I felt it again. I left the washcloth on my stomach and closed my eyes as I lay in the thick layer of bubbles. I tuned into that strange coldness of the presence and heard my name being whispered. I concentrated harder and felt the first touch. It lightly ran the path I had just washed and stopped at my stomach. Invisible fingers traced my wet skin and a cold sensation followed their path. The light went out as the room was plunged into darkness.

The ghost hand went up between my breasts and wrapped around my neck. If I'd been a normal girl I would've screamed, but instead I focused on the source of this trick. I put up a mental block after I reached toward the power that sought me. Pain danced through my skull as the source blocked my path. I relaxed in the water and forced this presence from me.

Male laughter rang in my ears.

"Who are you?"

"You'll soon find out."

Then something pierced my neck. I jerked up, touched my neck and found a drop of blood on my finger. What the hell? The presence disappeared just as Perseus knocked on the door.

"What happened? Are you okay?"

I drew my knees up to my chest and called him in.

He sank by the tub and looked at me. "What just happened?"

"I felt something and the voice was back again. Whoever it was had a strong barrier up because I couldn't see him. I asked who he was but he laughed and said I'd soon find out."

"You have blood on your neck. How did that happen?"

I wiped away the blood as I explained the pricking sensation I felt, and then reached for my robe on the floor.

Perseus got up and turned his back as I wrapped the robe around my slick body and pulled out the stopper. I watched the pink tinted water retreat down the drain and he started to pace across the bathroom floor.

"It had to be someone with a lot of power to get to me, but it'd take another person with extreme power to boost this being into a shapeless form that could touch people. And it hurts to see this man. I have never had this happen before and I need to understand it in order to stop it."

I touched Perseus' arm to stop his pacing and made him look at me. "Tell me what you think."

"I agree with you on the premise that someone is searching for you and he holds a power that we don't have. Our abilities and shared DNA will let us do this to each other but not with outsiders. Unless more power is involved than we think. We both agree that it's a man and he obviously wants you. We'll pool our resources to find a way around this block and destroy whoever he is and whatever power he's using. Have you met anyone new lately?"

I told him about running into the normal, human photographer. He nodded and pulled me to his chest.

"This means that you'll be coming with me to Louisiana next week. You need your herbs anyway, and we'll ask Bambara about this while we're there. Maybe she can find this person, or at least point us in the right direction."

"Sure, why not? I know my boss will tweak my schedule so I can."

I smiled and let the tension leave my body.

"Okay, we'll work out the schedule and you can call Bambara with the details of what's going on. I'll call the real estate agent and see which nights are better for him to meet us over there. Now go to bed and we'll finish the details tomorrow."

* * * *

I was on the schedule to work but Danya was off, so Perseus covered the bar. On slow nights like these, we pooled our resources and let people have some free time. I had to admit that it was cute seeing him get ogled as he worked the bar.

The night was good, for a slow night, so we didn't bother with breaks. It wasn't like we actually needed them. We had one fight and I saw it before it started so Perseus was able to control it before it got physical.

As I was leaving, I could sense an evil hovering around, but couldn't see whom it was. I wondered if my age had finally caught up to me. These new feelings confused me and I'd have to add it to the list of things to mention to Bambara when we met next week.

The plan was to leave Thursday night and come back Sunday night. We were staying just outside the French Quarter area at our usual hotel and they knew us, and what we were, there. Bambara was a short drive away from the hotel and I had called her earlier to tell her of our plans. She knew before I told her, of course, and said she already had my things prepared. She knew I had something on my mind and that we'd discuss it in person on Friday night.

My conversation with Bambara made me wish that I could take Danya to meet her, but right now I feared showing Danya too much of our lives. I knew it hurt her for me to turn down her requests to spend time together outside of work down so I'd gone out a few times for an early dinner and that had seemed to pacify her.

I still felt the dark presence around me as I approached the house, but saw no one. I did my vampire run around the block, and still felt nothing. The eerie quiet let me know that it was indeed a vampire. They were the obvious choice since they knew how fast to move to keep from being detected and how best to track someone. I just couldn't determine if it was a threat to me or not.

I knew there were other vampires around, but we hardly ever came in contact with them. Most vampires were loners and lived by their own rules, and most didn't see eye to eye. They were vain, power hungry, and determined to victimize the weak. A few had even told Perseus that we were crazy for living as we do, but that didn't change how we felt about our lives. The ones Perseus had been in contact with and respected had taught us a few tricks to blending in with humans that had been helpful in these long years together.

I walked the rest of the way home and knew I was being followed, but also knew they'd show themselves in time. Maybe they were simply curious about my life or maybe about Perseus. I didn't feel as if I was being threatened, so I went under the assumption that I could relax. By the time I got home, I could still feel the presences hovering in the near distance.

I stopped on the porch and reached out to it and said, "I know you're there."

I heard nothing after that, so I went inside to pour myself a drink of blood from the fridge. On tense nights like this I mixed my wine with a little blood, just to give myself a boost. I didn't require the herbs when I did this since the blood was directly involved.

By the time I took a shower and slid into bed, I no longer felt the presence outside. But I somehow knew he'd be back. I also didn't think it was as trained as I, or had any special powers. He knew whom I was and where to find me, but didn't want to be confronted. *How odd.* But then again, vampires were not known to be straightforward or honest in their doings.

I concentrated on Perseus and saw him as he went to feed on his prey. I hated to interrupt, but needed him to know about the male vampire stalking me. It'd be interesting if Perseus caught him when he came home. Perseus wasn't as amused as I was about that image, but I told him I was fine and would see him later. He knew I'd call him if anything strange were to happen, plus he'd use his own powers to search the area while he came back home as well.

I refused to be scared in my own home, let alone anywhere else, and it was hard to surprise me. I tried to let things go and see what developed, since I wasn't in any position to force anyone into making their plans known. It had taken many years to be this way but I found that letting the chips fall where they may, so to speak, made my existence easier. I fell asleep knowing that all would be shown to me, eventually.

* * * *

The wine spiced blood had thankfully led to a peaceful sleep without any visions or unwanted presences. Once awake, I wanted to inform Danya of my plans for the weekend. And while I did, I had to admire the way she dealt with the male customers. There were nights when I'd point out good guys at the bar, but she rarely even gave her number out unless she saw them a few times first. And even then she only indulged when she felt in bad need of some wild sex. I was all for a good tumble but had never had one myself. I had only been as far as what some would consider second base and that was enough for me. As it was I hadn't even been kissed in thirty years. But it truly wasn't a concern of mine. I just hoped that when the right guy comes along I'd know it. Maybe then I wouldn't end up being a virgin spinster at four hundred years old. I giggled at that thought.

Danya seemed happy about the trip.

"You'll be at the same hotel as last time, right?"

"Yes, it's the same hotel. The contact numbers are written on Perseus' desk calendar, plus you can call us on our cell phones. I'll work every night before then and I'll be here Monday night to tell you all about the trip and the new location."

"This is exciting. I want to be there for the opening, like I was for the one in Atlanta."

We had shared a crazy weekend for the Atlanta grand opening, since it'd been a nightclub. The entire staff, including Danya and I, had dressed up as go-go dancers, and the night had been a total success, as any business Perseus ran was prone to be. It still amazed me that he could own four businesses and be getting a fifth. I had a good feeling about the place in Louisiana and was excited about heading over there.

I got through work that day okay but felt that same presence half way through the night. It was the same one as last night so I kept my eyes open for anyone who looked suspicious. I was locking up the kitchen door and heading home when I smelled him. It was a blend of polished wood and cigars, but much older. I turned around, prepared myself, but was alarmed by the unexpected vampire who stood before me.

Jean Luc stood on the other side of the road. He nodded at me. I nodded back. It was a stand off. He smiled, bowed deeply and then vanished with vampire speed. Apparently he just wanted me to know it was him and we both knew he'd be back.

This brought up a list of things to be concerned about. When had he been turned? Who had done it? Why was he here? Was he the one who'd been in my bathroom the other night? Why had he not talked to me? Was he going to attack me? I considered these questions as I walked.

When I got home I sat on the porch and waited until Perseus came home. He knew something was wrong but I kept telling myself not to be distressed as of yet. This certainly didn't bode well with Jean Luc being part of the crew that had changed my life so very long ago.

Jean Luc being a vampire was okay, if he intended to leave me alone. But if he came for some sort of revenge then I'd have to kill him. I told Perseus what had happened and he got very quiet. We sat on the porch for a while and thought through our line of questions we wanted to ask him if given the chance, but neither would have any answers until Jean Luc decided to reveal his intentions.

"Do you see anything going on with Jean Luc?" Perseus finally asked me.

"No, and that's weird because I can't see anything about any of this. I know when he's watching me but nothing else. No motives or intentions. And if I try too hard to find out then I get a blinding headache until I stop. I'd feel better if I knew why he's here and what his intentions are."

"We'll have to figure this out. And fast. We don't need a sneak attack and we can't afford to ruin what we've got going on here."

"I'll keep my mind open and let you know if I see anything. I know you'll do the same."

"Yes, of course. I'm not comfortable with any of this, even if you don't sense any threatening vibes from him. Too many strange occurrences are going on and I don't like it one bit."

I patted his knee and got up to go inside.

"Pers, we'll get through this. We always do."

He just nodded. I sighed and went upstairs for my shower. Jean Luc was outside again, I could tell by the scent that wafted through my cracked bathroom window. I sensed when Perseus went outside to investigate. I rushed my shower but neither was there by the time I headed toward my bedroom door. I decided to work on the clothes that I was making, just to keep my mind off of these unsettling events.

Somewhere in the early morning, after the clothes had been set aside, I had a dream. I saw the tavern that I'd grown up in and Jean Luc was there. None of my family was around and we were sitting at the old bar with me standing behind the counter, like I'd have done back then.

"What do you want?"

"I heard you were here, so I was curious as to how you were living your life," he said as he drank a glass of blood.

"I'm fine, as you know, and have adjusted quite well."

"So I see. You and your brother have quite a life here. You haven't aged much; you're still very beautiful. I also see that you're more talented in your gift than before. However, you didn't see me coming, did you?"

"Yes, I've learned a lot along the way. Four hundred years will do that to you. Thank heavens we talk better than we used to. You seem to have aged a little more than I did. When were you changed?" I wiped the bar down as we spoke.

"I was changed twenty years after you and it wasn't by the captain," he avoided my gaze.

Curious.

"Someone else did it? Did you want this to happen or were you attacked as well?"

"Someone else did it and yes, I wanted it. I knew what the captain was and didn't care. I wanted to live forever. When I was offered the chance to be immortal, I was glad to have it happen."

"Do you have any other information? Like who made you and why you looked me up?"

"As I said, I was curious. A woman changed me and she did it to get revenge against the one who'd made her. It seemed he was neglecting her, so I was turned and became her lover as well. I was fine with the arrangement and now I'm working for someone who does not make me hide what I am as you and your brother do. You know, it's interesting how things have changed but other things have stayed the same. You're still beautiful, powerful and intriguing. And I'm still first mate, in many ways."

"So, you're still sailing under someone else's flag? Do I know your current employer or the woman who changed you?"

"They are of no importance. This is between you and me."

"I'd like to know your intentions. I'd hate for this to get ugly after all these years."

He leaned over and clasped my fingers. He brought them to his lips and gave them a cold kiss before saying, "I'd rather fuck ya than kill ya, my lady."

I gently pulled, trying to get free, but he held on tight.

"I'm sorry but that option is not available to you or anyone else at this time."

He smiled. "Do you mean to tell me that you still haven't had a lover?"

If I could have, I would've blushed at his bold question.

"No one has been given the opportunity and that's fine with me."

I finally succeeded in pulling my fingers away as he got up from the bar.

"That's quite a shame, keeping a body like yours to your self. If you happen to change your mind, let me know. I'm sure I'll be easy to find." Then he vanished.

I woke up and looked around to see if I was alone. A quick mental search showed Perseus was in bed asleep, so I didn't want to wake him up. Nothing was going to happen right now, so I figured it'd wait until tonight when we went to work to tell him what had happened.

Chapter Three

I was shaken awake, and sat straight up in a panic thinking Jean Luc had gotten me, but calmed once I saw that it was only Perseus. Only then did I hear my alarm going off on the table. When I glanced at it, I was surprised to see the lateness of the hour.

"Oh shoot! What happened?" I jumped out of bed.

"I've been hearing the alarm for a while, so I'm glad I came to check on you. You never sleep late. Are you okay?" He sat down on my rumpled covers as I grabbed clothes for work.

"I'm fine. I just had a dream about Jean Luc and it was hard to sleep after that."

I ran to the bathroom and started getting dressed when he knocked on the door. I clasped my bra and was clothed enough to open the door to him. He sat on the toilet seat as I continued to get ready.

"Tell me what you saw."

We both knew it wasn't an average dream, so I told him everything that was said. I had his full attention. Once I finished, he was silent for a moment, pronounced he'd walk me to work in a minute, and then abruptly left my suite.

I ran a wet brush through my hair, smudged on my liner, and then grabbed my bag as I headed to meet him at the front door. He smiled at me, opened the door for us and securely locked it shut behind us. The minute I walked outside, I immediately sensed something and looked around us. Perseus became tense beside me and looked around as well. He, however, didn't know what, or rather *who*, I was sensing. I smiled as I realized it was the same guy I'd run into with my rare cup of coffee. He was across the street with a camera around his neck.

"What's up with the guy? Do you know him?"

I whispered, "That's the guy I bumped into on the sidewalk outside our house."

I was focused enough to mentally sense that he was indeed a professional photographer in his early thirties. And he was staring straight at us.

He was standing in the general direction of where we were headed, so there was no sense avoiding him. I said hello and he smiled a gorgeous smile at me. He had a dimple in his left cheek but the large rimmed sunglasses he had on made it hard to see his eyes.

I sensed that he was happy to see me, and I was surprised by that emotion. But then his mood changed as he saw my brother. Perseus just nodded at him, keeping the mood somber.

"I didn't think I'd see you again," he said as he turned his camera off.

"We're local."

"Then you must work and live around here, since you're on foot. I'm new to town and haven't gotten the feel of it yet."

"There's a great bar on East Harris. You could always check it out."

Perseus grabbed my elbow. "Honey, we're late and need to get moving."

"Ok. Sorry. I have to get going. I'm running late and my boss will be mad at me if I don't get a move on."

The photographer stopped smiling and looked from my brother to me.

"Sorry to have kept you."

"See you around," I said as Perseus pulled me down the street toward work.

I waited until we were out of earshot to snap at Perseus. "Why were you so rude to that man?"

"We've had some strange things going on lately and this guy has bumped into you twice since this all started. He may seem harmless, but I don't want to take any chances. If you run into any more people or have any other issues that pop up, you need to get my attention."

"Okay," I agreed as I didn't want to argue with him about this and we had reached the building.

Danya was in my face the moment I got through the front door.

"What happened? You're *never* late."

I sighed and got ready for my customers.

"I'm fine. I had a rough night and slept through my alarm. It's no big deal."

"Well, you slept through your alarm, look stressed, *and* it seems like your brother is ready to punch something. I'd call that a big deal"

Looking at Perseus, I knew she was right. He was normally pretty laid back but recently he was more tense than I had ever seen him.

"To be honest with you, I've had some weird occurrences lately. And someone from my past has shown up. The timing in all of this is strange, and Perseus is just worried about me. It'll all pass and things will be back to normal in no time. I know it."

I smiled at her to ease her mind, but it was clear she wasn't buying it.

"Look, if you need anything, please let me know. I don't care if I'm asleep or lined with customers, do you hear me?"

She was shaking her finger at me. It was sweet to know that a normal person was worried about an immortal with super powers.

Two hours into the night I felt someone tap me on my shoulder. I turned to see that it was the photographer. His warm smile crinkled his eyes and made his dimple appear.

"Do you tell fortunes here, or are you just dressed for the ambience?" He reached out for my empty hand.

"Yes, I'm a fortune teller and this outfit comes with the job. But I do dress like this all the time."

"I'm Justin Storm," he said as he kissed my hand.

I whispered, "Andromeda Ortiz."

"Do you mind?" He asked as he waved toward the chair opposite me.

"Not at all. Do you want tarot cards or your palm read?" I asked as I opened my mind to him.

"Let's do my palm this time," he said as he put out both hands, palms up.

"This time?" I asked before touching his hands.

"Yes, I like the place. It may even become a regular hangout for me. That is, if your boyfriend doesn't mind."

He tilted his head to look behind me. I turned to see Perseus staring back at us. He was leaning against the bar with his arms folded sternly over his puffed out chest. I laughed and looked back at my customer.

"You can do as you wish, since that man is my twin brother and as such defiantly *not* my boyfriend."

He wiped his hand over his brow in mock relief. "I'm glad to hear it. I thought I was about to get thrown out of my first bar for flirting with a gorgeous gypsy."

"You'll only get thrown out if you piss me off. Fair warning. But for now, you're safe. Ignore his looks and let's get these palms read."

I chose to ignore the comment about flirting, because working in a bar means constant comments, some nice and some not so nice. I grasped both of his large hands and immediately saw flashes in my mind. It made the room spin and I held on tight to his hands as I fought to reign in the speeding images. I closed my eyes and absorbed the tornado of moving pictures as they began to slow to a mild gust.

I saw him at my house, softly kissing me in the dark at the front door. Then I saw him holding my hand as we walked the silent streets. I saw him walking toward me at River Street and finally I saw him lying in my tumbled bed. I gasped at the last image, released his hands and inhaled a deep cleansing breath. He was looking at me as if he'd been struck by lightening.

"What was that?"

I could feel the energy in the air and apologized before grabbing his hands again. The visions still weren't over.

I saw him dying and there was blood everywhere. I was leaning over him with his damp head in my dust-coated lap as he took his last gasping breath. *Oh my God.* This man was to be my mate and he'd die because of it. And I couldn't tell when these things would happen. Some of it was covered in shadow, as if fate still held it in her firm hands. How could I see him die when I didn't even know his name? I slammed to the back of my chair and just stared at his shaking hands.

"Please explain to me why I feel like I just stuck my finger into a light socket?"

"I don't know. That's never happened before," I said as I looked around for Perseus.

"There was a rush of emotions, like I belonged with you. Please tell me you have this table rigged like some carnie side show?"

"No. Do you see any wires? Take the cover off of the table, if you need to. I really am a third generation fortuneteller and I received several visions when I touched you. I believe a portion of what you felt were my emotions being thrown back at you."

At that, Perseus finally came over to stand next to me. "You okay?"

I nodded and nudged my head toward the kitchen door. He understood and headed that way.

I looked at my customer. "I am truly sorry. Please give me a minute. I'll be back."

I started to get up but he reached out to grab my arm and stopped me.

"Please tell me what you saw."

I looked him straight in his troubled eyes. "I *will* be back. Please let me process this."

I moved as quickly as human eyes would let me.

Perseus was pacing outside as I leaned against the cold stonewall. It took me a minute to calm myself enough to tell Perseus all of what I'd seen. He was shocked at how vast the images had been over such a simple touch. He'd never had that happen before personally, but my powers were much stronger than his. I told him all of the visions I'd had, even the one about this man being my lover. He took it all in, and then fiercely hugged me.

"I felt your emotions hit and knew this was no ordinary vision. What do you want to do now?"

"You know I have to talk to him. I can't run from this. I'll tell him a portion of what I saw and see what happens. I'll compel him if I have to. We'll go from there."

Through my powers, I knew he was in there right now getting a drink from Danya, and I also saw she knew something was wrong for me to run outside. I'd have questions to answer no matter what I did.

"This is scary, but I know that it's the right thing to do. Just trust me on this."

I hummed an old gypsy tune softly to calm myself as I came up behind the man of my dreams and nightmares.

"Can you come outside with me for a minute?"

"Yes."

He finished his drink as I escorted him to a brick half wall across the street.

"I'm sorry for the way I handled that. This has never happened to me before. And most of what I saw was good. But you need to know that not all of it was." I avoided his gaze.

"Just tell me what you saw and we'll go from there."

"I saw us kissing, you holding my hand at my house, you walking me home and us as lovers."

"I see. But those are all good things. The bad part?"

"I know that I need to tell you what I saw. But this is going to be hard to absorb."

"Just tell me."

"I saw you die."

I waited for his reaction. He was very quiet and then jumped off the wall and began pacing.

"You saw me die. Okay. I need to know where, when and how."

I could only watch as I said, "I can only tell you that there was a lot of blood and that I was holding you when you drew your last breath. There's fuzziness around the image, as if it wasn't quite true yet."

"Everyone makes decisions that can change their destiny. So this can be avoided then, right?"

"Yes. Everyone can change their future by changing the decisions that lead up to it. I have regulars because of this. But the only thing that can stop this is if you stay away from me."

There. I'd said it.

"So, I die because of you but you don't know how or when?" It was commendable that he was seriously trying to rationalize this.

"Yes. And that's all I can tell you. I understand if you want to run away and never look back. I'm sorry."

"What makes you think that? Do you see me doing that? I've seen too much loss in my life to just take that as the gospel truth. I am master of my own destiny. I won't be going out like that."

He stood in front of me and I looked into his eyes. There it was, the truth of the matter. I see him with me until his death and then nothing else. For either of us.

Had I truly found my mate and was his death something we could avoid? I saw something in his eyes like determination, and he leaned closer to me.

He whispered, "I'm not sorry."

"For what?"

"You already know."

Then he kissed me. His lips were soft and a current ran through them as if we were electrified. He wasn't touching any other part of me and yet it was the best kiss I'd ever had. His mouth roamed over mine with softness and I knew we were both holding back, which only enhanced the electricity between us.

I saw more images as he slowly learned the finite details of my mouth. I saw us rolling in my bed, us riding in his car, us in my living room as we drank wine and then one of me gasping in bed. The last one was vague, strange, and it made me break the heart-stealing kiss. He leaned against the wall and simply stared at my face.

"I've never felt like that before."

"Me neither."

"No, you don't understand. I felt things just now. It was just like when you held my hands earlier. Did you feel it too?" He played with a strand of my hair that lay on my shoulder.

"Yes. I felt happiness, passion and then something strange. That's why I moved away."

"I felt all of those things too. It was like there was a live wire connecting us. And to be honest, I liked it. A lot. Do you do this to all the guys you kiss?"

"No. And trust me, there haven't been a lot of men in my life."

"Seriously? You must have them lined up somewhere."

I sighed, "No, really I don't. And there are things you need to know and understand about me. But it's too soon for all of that. I'm unique and I don't mean in the 'one of a kind' status. I'm a gypsy with special powers and have lived a very long time." As soon as this was out, I waited for his rejection. But it never came. Instead, he just looked at me.

"I knew you were special the first time I saw you. I even tried to take a picture of you that day, after you bumped into me. I thought I'd never see you again and wanted to capture the moment. But the photo didn't turn out. I guess that shows you just how affected I was at your beauty. I have the photo, but all I see is landscape and the side of a house. Definitely not my best work." He shook his head.

Little did he know the real reason why his photo didn't turn out.

I continued my speech. "Let's be realistic. I'm not what you're used to dealing with, on many different levels. I come with baggage and a unique lifestyle. I've already seen that you'll die if you continue to be around me and I can't have that on my soul. I care about your welfare without even knowing who you are. That's a lot to take in, too much. You really need to stay away from me. For your own benefit." I stepped away from him and held my hands behind my back as I fought my urge to reach out to him. I felt his emotions roll as well, and I excused myself. He grabbed my hand as I went to pass him. The touch shot currents up my arm. Was it always going to be like this with each other? Were we really that connected already?

"It's been a pleasure, milady." He bowed over my hand, and then let me go. I wanted him to run away from me and never leave me all in the same thought. Instead, I settled on the next best option—the truth.

"I'm going back to work and I want you to truly consider what I've told you tonight. I *cannot* have your death on my hands. I know you go with your gut, but so do I. I see passion and love but I can't escape the image of you dying. Please think long and hard. I truly hope to never see you again."

I walked away but heard him whisper. "You would miss me."

I stopped and looked at him over my shoulder and only said one word. "Yes."

* * * *

I held my head high as I walked back into the bar. I didn't chance a look back because I knew he wouldn't be there. I came up behind Danya and grabbed the first bottle of liquor on the shelf and I poured myself a double, swallowing it without a thought. The whole time I could tell Danya was dying to ask me what was wrong. But I just couldn't.

"Please give me some room and I promise to answer your questions when we close up. I've neglected my job long enough and need to get back to it. That goes for you as well, Perseus."

I knew he'd come up to the bar, so I brushed them both off at one time.

It was as if the Grim Reaper himself was beside me all night as I replayed Justin dying over and over again in my mind. I was sinking into a mental shutdown by closing time. Danya walked me out as Perseus stayed to finish the liquor inventory. She was quiet the first block, but I knew she needed answers.

"Go ahead and ask me, or do you intend to walk me all the way home?"

"I didn't think I'd get my answers unless I walked you home. There isn't enough time to get them all answered in such a short walk."

"Why don't we just take the long route to your car? Then you'll have more time to ask your questions. Besides, I'll enjoy the walk after working that table for three hours."

"Alright then. But brace yourself. Who is the guy you went outside with? What happened out there? Why did he not come back in? Why was Perseus watching you like a hawk all night? Did you really over sleep? What kept you up last night?"

She took a deep breath and waited for my answers.

"Justin Storm and he's the photographer that I ran into a while ago. I saw his future and it was both good and bad. He didn't like my response when I told him what I saw. Perseus knows something's wrong and is worried about me. Yes, I did. I had a very bad dream and couldn't get back to sleep afterward." Danya paused, ingesting all the information I just delivered. After a moment, she seemed to accept what I'd said.

"Okay. It must've been one hell of a vision if you both reacted like that. What's going on? Can I help you?"

"What I saw of his future was entangled with mine. We're together, but something happens to him because of being around me. I told him to stay away from me but he didn't take my warning seriously. You know people either think I'm a freak or a fake, so him thinking that he can change my visions was a bit unusual to me."

"Are you going to tell me what you saw?"

"I can, but you have to keep it to yourself. I don't like sharing personal stuff. But it does help having a friend to talk to."

She nodded in agreement so I continued. "I saw him as my lover and then get hurt because of me. He was bleeding to death."

"Wow. That's harsh. I'm happy that you finally found a man for yourself, but it makes it complicated if you know he's going to get hurt. So you told him to stay away from you and he left?"

"Yes and no. I told him to stay away, but he's not afraid of what I saw. He thinks it's all going to change once we spend more time together. And he's not thinking about the consequences. I can't have his death be because of me. But at the same time I feel a bond with this man that I've never had with anyone else. How can I wrap myself in the possibility of love when his doom is at my hands? What would you do?"

"Death? That changes things. That's intense. I guess, if it were me, I'd tell him to back off. But if he didn't, then I'd go ahead with the relationship and see if you could change your vision. If it gets worse, then you walk away and be glad you had him for the short time you did."

"Yes, but that could also be said for being with him until his death. I've lost too many loved ones to tragedy. I don't want it to happen anymore. If I can stop it, then I have to do my best to keep him safe."

"I agree. But this is a rare man, and you owe it to yourself to see what you can do. Either way, you'll have regrets. You'll regret loving him and losing him, whether it be by his death or you pushing him away for his own protection. You need to think about what you can live with. If he comes back, then see what your visions have in store and go from there."

I gave thought to her words and agreed with them. "I can do that. *If* he comes back."

"You know he will. *I* would. And if he doesn't, then he wasn't worth it anyway."

I nodded in agreement as we got to her car. I hugged her and said goodnight.

I pondered her advice as I meandered back home.

She was right. If it was worth it then he'd come back. And I'd take that as a positive sign and try to see if his future changed. I wanted the passion from my vision but not if it cost him his life. So I'd leave it up to Fate and see where she led me.

Being a vampire made me see death on a different level. I saw many people die and only a select few ever came back. Fate chose her victims and blessed her friends. I could keep him as a friend and see if that changed his tragic ending or I could walk away and know I'd saved him. He was mortal after all, and our time together would always be limited.

I'd never revealed myself to any man that I'd dated and wouldn't start now. Maybe it'd be easier if I could find a vampire mate or lover. I'd deeply consider that option, especially after all I'd been through. I'd resolved to talk to Perseus about his experiences, and knew he'd find that conversation incredibly amusing when I did. But I also knew he would at least be honest with me.

When I got home I asked if he would meet me downstairs. We sat down on each side of the den sofa as both of us drank blood-laced vodka. I didn't know where to start, so decided on jumping right in.

Chapter Four

"I have a decision in front of me, and I want to know some of your past experiences so I can make an informed decision."

"Ask away. I have no secrets in my life."

"In my vision I saw myself as Justin's lover and I want it to come true. But not if it'll get him killed."

"Okay, I see the dilemma. You told him about the visions when you went outside, even the bad part, right?"

"Yeah, but I didn't tell him all of the gory details."

"What did you leave out?"

"I saw us doing normal everyday things; us kissing, and making love, but nothing that showed why he dies. I wish I could see more. What if something's wrong with me?" The more I talked, the more panicked I became. But Perseus calmed me down, as he always did.

"I don't think anything's wrong with you. It's just not meant to be seen yet. What do you feel for this mortal?"

He met my eyes and I showed him what I felt when Justin kissed me, my smiles at Justin being by my side, and the tears of feeling his last breath as I held Justin to me. I was overcome by my instant and unwavering feelings for Justin. Perseus sighed when it was over.

"You've never felt that before. Do you want him as your first lover? I'm sure you've thought over the decisions you have to make in regards to whether he can handle the truth about us or not. But no matter what, you'll wonder if you made the right choice."

"How did you handle the lovers that didn't know the truth?"

"I've only had a handful that knew my true self. I've had one-night stands and I've had affairs, and most of these women where clueless. Only one lover had to be compelled afterward, for my own safety. The ones that worked out were glad to have me and I took care of them because of it."

"This is the first man I've ever been drawn to sexually."

"I've always wondered if you'd find a mate. If you were mortal, people would wonder if you were gay," he laughed at his joke. "You see, I see love in different shapes, colors and forms. I'm not trivial or analytical when I'm drawn to someone. I've been drawn to men as well as to women, even though I've never taken a man as a lover. I'm told that's because vampires feel things stronger than any mortal ever could."

I was shocked and wondered why he'd even told me his true feelings.

"Andromeda, I know this is foreign to you but it's who I am. I believe that your power has had you in such a singular focus you haven't been open to sexual needs. I lost my virginity when I was sixteen so I was sexually active before we were changed. You didn't, and maybe that's why it's not in you to be so susceptive. Maybe this will open you to more physical experiences."

"I'm not sure, but I'm leery about the amount of drama involved in this situation. I don't want a relationship based on lies, but I know I have to hide things on some level. I'd love to tell Danya and Justin about us but I know you're against that. Doesn't it ever bother you not to share your life with the people close to you?"

"Yes, it does and I learned a valuable lesson from what happened with Valentina. She killed herself to keep from being like us. You know how much of me died with her. I don't regret my time with her, but I could've saved us both a lot of heartache if I'd told her the truth before we'd gotten serious. I would've known that she wasn't open to our lifestyle and would've compelled her before things had gotten out of hand. But Fate had destined for me to lose her either way and I feel that she didn't really love me because true love surpasses immortality"

I knew that even if he'd told her the truth, it still would've ended at that moment. Her beliefs were just too different.

"I agree with you, in part. But still, you had love, even if brief. Justin thinks he can change what I saw and wants to see where this relationship will lead us. I can't get too far into this without telling him the truth. If I have to compel him, then so be it, but I'm more worried about him being injured than of us having a relationship."

"Yes, I have a problem with you telling people about us because it doesn't just affect your life, it affects mine, too. But I can't make any of these decisions for you, so do what you feel you have to do. If I were you, I wouldn't turn down the possibility of happiness, especially when we're immortal."

"You? Giving me advice on love? That's funny."

"I know what you're thinking. But I meant that comment for your own life, not mine. I've loved and lost and I'm not ready to make that commitment again. I'll take love in small doses and put the rest of my energy into my work. At least my business can see me into the future. Love can visit when needed."

"You pass up love all the time. You tell me to grab what I can and just keep living, but you ignore the love that's offered to you. I know there are women who'd literally give up their souls to be your mate and yet you turn the other way. I know Valentina ripped your heart to shreds and I wish I could take that pain away. You'd be with her right now if she'd been more open minded about our lives. But she wasn't and as a result, you now have blinders on when it comes to anything close to your heart. But you can't live forever with that mentality. You should take your own advice and keep your eyes open to someone who can be with you through your eternity."

"I will not allow myself to make the same mistake again. If you're the only woman in my life, then so be it. I'll survive on distant sexual encounters and a few friends. I can't offer a shattered heart to someone who deserves better."

"If you never offer, then no one will ever accept. I love you and only want the best for you, but this has to stop. You can't condemn yourself because she made the wrong decision."

He straightened his back. "I will *not* go through that again. It'd have to be someone special for me to even consider changing my mind."

"I still stand by what I said. You should be more open to things, just as you're telling me to be. If Justin comes back, then I'll try to talk him into leaving me alone. But if he stays, then I'll trust in Fate."

I swallowed the rest of my drink and hugged Perseus.

"I love you, you hypocritical ass."

* * * *

I woke up the next day, or rather, night, with the determination to have a good shift at work and dressed to fit my mood in a blue velvet gown that I had made a couple of months ago. I added my black flats, a long necklace of red jade, matching drop earrings and a chunky red jade bangle bracelet. My hair was pulled to the side using a black scarf. All set, I grabbed my bag and strolled through the front door. It was a gorgeous night and it seemed that nothing bad would happen.

When I walked in, Danya was already set up for the night and admired my outfit.

"Nice dress! Can you make me one in a copper shade?"

"I can probably order the copper but I do have a deep russet color ready now, if you're interested in that?"

"All I need to know is two things. One, would it look good with my coloring? And two, would I look weird in that style?"

"How about I let you try it on and see what you think. Then I can see if there are any changes I need to make while you have it on. I think the russet would be great with your hair and skin tone. I ordered it on a whim two months ago and it has been sitting around collecting dust ever since."

"Okay, but let's make it quick."

The restrooms were being cleaned, so I suggested Perseus' office to try the thing on.

"If you're sure he's not here, then okay," she said as we walked into his quiet office.

I stripped off the dress and waited for her to get out of her leggings and tunic blouse. She was in a smoky gray satin strapless bra with matching thong panties. There was a two-inch scar across her left side, right under her strapless bra.

She saw me noticing it and just shrugged before saying, "Some monsters live only to hurt others, but I at least survived to see him die."

"Did an old love do this to you?" I handed the dress over to her and felt her pain in the brief touch of her hand.

"Yes. He tried to stab me in the back. Literally. I moved at the last second and it kept him from slicing into my spine. He was high on meth and thought I'd hidden his stash from him. Apparently, he needed it bad enough to kill me."

She pulled the velvet into place and it looked great, even with it being a few inches too short for her. The waistline emphasized her hips and the straps brought attention to her square shoulders. I knew exactly how to alter it to be more flattering and we were discussing the details as I felt Perseus come into the bar. She had taken off the dress and was handing it to me when the door opened. He stepped in and his gaze took in Danya's semi-nude body in front of him.

She dropped the dress when she saw him and time seemed to stop. I had no idea who was emitting what, but the air was ripe with raw need, embarrassment, shock, and awe. I didn't move for fear that I'd break the spell. Perseus came to first and reached down to pick up my forgotten dress. I accepted it without a word as his eyes never left Danya's body. I slipped it on and saw Danya turn scarlet as she grabbed her clothes as a shield before her body, but the damage had already been done. She would've been better off just to dress in silence or even make a joke of the situation, but she didn't. I decided to make the joke for her.

"I get someone naked in your office and you decide to walk in? What kind of brother are you?"

"I guess you should've locked the door. Besides, if anyone gets naked in my office, then I have the right to enjoy it."

He smiled and I felt Danya's embarrassment grow. She had a gorgeous blush covering her skin. I enjoyed this moment, but only at the satisfaction I got from knowing he wanted her as much as she wanted him.

"Well, no harm no foul."

I shrugged and winked at Danya when she finally looked at me. She wasn't sure if I'd known he would walk in, but intended to ask me when we were along again. I nodded at her in answer and she frowned at me. I shrugged again and she broke the tension.

"Boss, do you mind turning around so I can get dressed?"

"Yes, I do. I've already seen most of that gorgeous body so why try to hide it now?"

"A gentleman would turn around," she countered as she still held her clothes against her blushing body.

"I never claimed to be a gentleman." He gave her a heated look. "I suggest you get dressed quickly because our liquor rep will be in here in three minutes."

She knew he wasn't joking with that, so she hurriedly got dressed. He sat down in his big chair while she dressed silently beside him. He was kind enough to pretend not to watch her, but I knew he was looking at her through the top of his lashes-- and he liked what he saw. I giggled when I noticed that he had a great view of her curvy butt. There was a small Monarch butterfly tattoo on her right hip.

"I guess we've done well enough to need more alcohol?" I said after a moment. Business would get him to focus.

"Yes, and I need to make sure we have enough through the weekend since we won't be here to order more. Danya, you were told we're leaving tomorrow night, right?" Perseus said as he pretended to be going over the papers on his desk.

"Yes," she grunted as she yanked her top into place.

Slipping on her silver flats, I felt her get a grip on her embarrassment.

"We have enough vodka for two nights, but we're low on draft beer."

"I'm glad you mentioned beer. I was given some suggestions on new seasonal ones to try. What do you think of trying that for a month?"

"I say we go for it. We do have several eclectic tastes with our regulars. We could put up a sign to advertise them. Get me a list of what you want to try and I'll draw something up on the chalk board by the bar."

"Good idea. I'll give you the list before we leave tonight and you can work on it tomorrow when you come in."

He nodded and she took that as a dismissal and went to greet our rep. I followed behind her but he stopped me right before I left the room.

"Yes?"

"You knew I was coming through that door."

"Yep. Just like you knew that Danya was in here. So let's not pretend."

"I knew you guys were in here but not to change clothes, which was an interesting thing to walk in on."

"You liked it."

"Yes, I did. And one day I'll ask her about what I saw."

"I'm sure she'll tell you, if you ask."

With that, I walked out to the door and to the rep.

I supposed feeling guilty would be the appropriate response after what happened, but this tension between them was too delicious. And besides, Danya wouldn't be mad for long. She tried to never hold a grudge, even if it hurt to learn her lesson. I walked to the bar where she already had a couple of customers lined up as the rep was leaving and went behind the bar to get a glass of water. I whispered in her ear.

"Yes, I knew he was about to walk in, but I couldn't stop it."

I heard a humph from her and she said, "I figured that. Would you have tried?"

"Honestly? No. I think he needed to see that body of yours. And I think you liked the reaction it had on him. What's not to like about any of it?"

"That's true, I guess. I was going out of my mind when he saw me, but the look in his eyes sure did curl my toes."

"Then it was worth the blush."

"Never *ever* tell him that."

He couldn't keep his eyes off of her the rest of the night. At one point he was even envisioning her in her gray satin lingerie again. He'd had to shake the image from his mind.

I knew this moment would change things between them and was glad for it. I hoped he'd sweep her off for some hot sex, just so they could see if it was worth it. It made me think of the vision I had of Justin and I in bed. I wondered how our kind dealt with sex and super strength. I knew to keep it to a minimum when doing everyday things, but I'd guess that lovemaking put you in a different frame of mind. This could be very interesting, or very dangerous.

I went about my night and didn't notice anything strange until an hour before closing. I felt him before he came in the door and alerted Perseus to my feelings. No one was at my table, so I knew this conversation would be more private. Jean Luc limped right up to my table and flopped down on the empty chair opposite me. Perseus came to stand beside my chair.

"To what do I owe this appearance?"

He smiled the smile of a hungry crocodile and chuckled at me.

"Well?" Perseus asked him.

"Now now, can't we have a nice little chat without getting antsy?"

"I haven't seen you in a long time and I don't remember it being very pleasant when we last did. So why don't you tell us what's going on." Perseus was perturbed.

"I just wanted to catch up with you. There's nothing wrong with that, mate," Jean Luc said, getting more comfortable in his chair.

I knew something was up his sleeve, regardless of his claims otherwise, so I tried a different approach.

"So, how long have you been a true carnivore?"

Jean Luc stopped smiling. "Oh, that happened in 1574. And not by the same one that made you two."

"I would've thought that the captain had taken care of that so he could keep his first mate forever."

"No, he liked me as a lackey, so he thought our arrangement was fine as it was. I ran into one of his other pets and was changed just to keep me around. I have since found employment with an entrepreneur who sails around the world."

"Well, it seems to have been good for you. You only look about fifty-five and have a spring in your step."

Vampirism wasn't able to correct a defect that happened prior to the change. It simply froze you as you were at that time in your mortal life. It gave him a more sinister stance and went well with the scar across his right eye courtesy of Perseus.

"I can see that you still have your gifts."

Perseus spoke up. "You know full well that our gifts are still intact."

"Yes. I also know that you two have done quite well over the years. Perseus, you've made lots of money and have kept your sister in good standards."

"No one keeps her. She can do as she pleases and always has."

"Yes, of course she can. I meant no offense. It's just rare to see siblings stay together after all these years. You two must have a very strong bond."

"We do. And we stand up for each other, no matter what happens to cross our paths."

"I see. Well, I just wanted to say hello face to face. Even though I'd already checked you both out, as you know. One of the first things I had to adjust to when I changed was the heightening of my psychic abilities to the point that I was able to tune in to anyone, given enough time and strength."

"I would've thought that it was the need for drinking blood. It was for me," I said.

"No, being a pirate got me used to spilling blood, lass. I also did whatever it took to get the booty, in the end." He leered at me as he spoke.

"Things have indeed changed after all these years, but some things stay the same. Like our principles," I snapped back at him.

"Mores the pity, my lovely lass."

Perseus gripped the chair with white knuckles in his growing anger. "So what were you expecting to get from this impromptu visit?"

"My employer happens to have business in the area, so I have a little free time while we wait on some items to arrive. I might even be stopping by from time to time." Jean Luc got up from the chair. "Maybe I'll even send a couple of my friends by. I think they'll like the ambience of this place."

I concentrated on his words and saw two people's forms, a woman and a man. I could tell by their energy that they were both vampires but saw no faces as they exited a ship in the cover of darkness. I felt a strong connection between the three and thought that the woman may have been the one that had changed Jean Luc. The more I tried to see their faces the more painful it became. I turned to Jean Luc as he stood behind me and gave him my full attention.

"*Cherie*, you'll get an awful headache if you search like that."

He walked away while I absorbed his words. Perseus came back after he made sure that Jean Luc had left, looking more stressed than I'd even seen him.

"He knows something we don't and I don't like that," he said as he moved to sit in Jean Luc's vacant chair.

I saw him close his eyes as he tried to focus on Jean Luc, but he frowned as he got the same headache that I was suffering.

"I see what he was referring to. Trying to focus on him or his friends will give you a headache. And that can only mean he has things to hide."

I leaned back and sighed. Danya came up with a tray and handed both of us a glass of clear liquid.

"This is a new brand of vodka; the rep gave us a small bottle. By the look of you two, I figured you could use the sample." We saluted each other and downed the liquor. It was pretty good for not being blood. I nodded to her and Perseus gave her back our glasses before she walked away.

I took a few more customers before we closed up and even had time to clean up the bar with Danya. I was surprised when she didn't ask one single thing about our curious visitor. I locked up with Perseus and Danya, and then we all walked together for a block.

Before she parted ways, Danya hugged me. "You'll let me know if you need anything, right?"

"Yes. Don't worry, we'll be fine."

Perseus hugged her next and held on a little too long for a normal boss. I acted like I didn't notice.

"Call us if you have any problems," he said as he kissed her on the forehead.

She was dumb struck. We left her with that expression stuck on her face as we walked toward the house. Perseus did a quick disappearing act when we were out of her sight. He was checking to make sure no strangers were following Danya, especially after our visitor tonight. This concern for her safety spoke volumes about his growing feelings for my best friend. He was creeping out of his comfort level as he got closer to blurring the line of their employee-boss relationship. I said nothing as he whipped back to walk home with me.

When we got to the house, the clothes were packed in a whirl of colors as we set to keep our schedule. The traditional ten-hour driving time was a push for our sleeping arrangements, but with us being vampires, we usually did the trip in five to six hours.

As we drove, I thought about Justin and his possible reaction to me when, or if, I told him about being a vampire. Tapping into his thoughts, I could sense Justin sitting on a balcony in deep thought. He was thinking about what I'd told him. He frowned. This was hard for him. He was volleying back and forth about what to do and knew there was more to me than just my powers. He had no idea. I left him to his thoughts as I decided to handle whatever decision he made.

Just as I shut off my internal image, I heard Perseus speak up. "He still hasn't decided."

"No, he hasn't," I agreed. "But he at least knows something is different about me, and so does Danya."

"Maybe we should compel them both?"

"I think it's time we trusted some people. Danya should be the first. Don't you think?"

"Do you realize how hard it'll be for us if she doesn't accept us? What if she freaks out? I think it'd be a nightmare to stay around her everyday if she rejects us."

"But what if she doesn't? You have to realize that she may be okay with this. She's had her own trauma and hasn't let it scar her life. What are you afraid of?"

"What if it turns out like it did with Valentina?" He said in a small voice.

"I know. And I'm sorry you're worried about that. But I honestly think she needs to know the truth. I'm prepared to go around you on this."

He frowned and his hands tensed on the steering wheel. I gave him a moment to compose himself and let him talk.

"You can't do that. She's involved in both of our lives and the business as well. You can't just snatch off the blindfold like that. Especially without my consent,"

"Yes, I can. And one day I will."

"Can you please at least wait a little longer before you do that? I need time before you change our little group."

"Yes. Fine. But if you wait too long, I'll tell her on my own. At that time, you'll have no choice but to face it."

Chapter Five

We drove the rest of the way in silence and got to the hotel just after midnight. We always stayed here because the owner happened to be a vampire from our time. He went by the name of Frank Reynolds but was born as Frances Reinhardt about five hundred years ago. He was stout, about five-feet-eight, and always had a smile in his eyes. You could never tell from his facial expressions if he was thinking something pleasant or something sinister, but he remained fiercely protective of our kind.

After we checked in at the front desk our bags were taken up for us as we went to say hello to Frank. He gave us both a glass of blood as we took a seat in his luxurious office. Because of his clientele, he kept items on hand that were not the usual hotel faire, such as bags of blood in the mini refrigerators. He also had an assortment of prostitutes that were available for anyone with more physical needs.

I didn't agree with this type of hired help, but I could see that he took care of his girls. He never took away their free will to say no to anyone. He'd even once told me that he'd found them on the streets and put them in a better working environment.

Frank loved gossip as much as his girls, but never repeated anything. He kept it all inside like his own personal soap opera. If he ever decided to write a book, we'd all fall prey to his well-informed words. Perseus filled Frank in on the new store and how Mythology was progressing. Frank, as always, offered his services for anything we needed for the new bar, which would be helpful when it came to hiring a new staff. After thanking him and wishing him a good sleep, we headed to our suite for some rest.

The petal soft sheets were turned down and I laid my customary pouches of soil under the mattress and pillow. I had crates of that same earth in my basement, enough to last us through our eternity together. I always imagined if anyone ever saw it they'd think I must be into gardening, which was amusing since the only things that grew for me were my fangs.

I said goodnight to my brother and left him working at the antique desk between our rooms. The approaching sunrise made me tired, but I had to indulge myself with a hot shower in my opulent bathroom. The shower had special massage heads that beat into my tough, vampiric skin. It was heavenly. I'd have to ask Frank where he got them so I could get them for the house.

Once tucked in bed, sleep came slowly and distressingly as I saw strange things floating through my head. I saw a ship with people coming off of it, a limo, and the back of a dark skinned man. The man was bald and tall as he walked toward the ship to shake hands with a man on the dock. I reached further into the image and saw a doll wrapped in sheer fabric, but no little girl to claim it. The limo drove off and I didn't see anything else except blackness.

I was startled awake with the feeling that someone was in the room with me. Something moved up my body, and moved the blanket with it. This was no ordinary nightmare; this was much more invasive. I mentally yelled for Perseus. He woke with a start and headed to my room. The movement stopped at my crotch and just circled for a moment, like some insane spinning top. It then shot up to my stomach and pressed down with enough pressure to sink me into the mattress. It fanned out across my midriff. I gasped.

I heard Perseus at the door as he shouldered it. It wouldn't budge. He shoved it as hard as possible, making the door splinter from the wooden frame, but still it would not break. I shrieked for him but another ghostly object stopped me and pressed down over my mouth, smothering my cry. My head reeled with the pain.

Perseus finally broke down the door and got to the bed where he saw that I was anchored to that spot. His vampire eyes saw through the dark to the impression on the tousled covers. He pried at the object on my stomach but he was systematically knocked backwards by the invisible force. I heard a maniacal laugh in my head as I failed at my attempt to remove the pressure to my captured body. The temperature in the bed increased, as if an electric blanket had been turned on the highest setting possible. I struggled to free myself from my invisible restraint, but to no avail. Perseus crept across the Berber carpet as I fought the oppressive heat and impossible pressure.

I centered my aching head and asked the presence again what it wanted.

"*You*" was the only reply.

Perseus must have heard it too because he dove on top of me to put a barrier between the ghost and I. He was easily knocked away again and a second hand encircled my straining neck. A familiar prick sank into my sweaty skin. My head pounded like a stampede of horses as I fought for control.

Then it happened. Wind that smelled of woods and herbs whipped around the room. I heard a comforting chant swell in the room, through the storm in my head. It swirled through before it settled on the inferno below my bending ribs. A flash of light went through the darkness. I was released from that monstrous hold and I was thrown against the cherry wood headboard, splintering it upon impact and landed with a thud on the bed. My headache faded as Perseus climbed to the edge of the now ruined bed. I held his hand as he turned on the bedside lamp.

"Your neck is bleeding."

I touched it and my finger came away with a single drop of dark blood, like before. But unlike before, I felt a hot sensation on my stomach. I yanked up my gown and saw there was a burn forming on my stomach in the shape of a large human hand. Something dark was entrenching into my life. The need to speak with Bambara was increasing with each unearthly event. She was the only person I knew of who could find and track this type of power. I had to find out what was targeting me because I strongly believed that it would kill me if it didn't get what it was after. Perseus paced as I looked around the room. There was a dent in the wall were Perseus' had been thrown. I knew it was Frank when I heard the shrill ring of the phone that had fallen during our scuffle.

"Is everything okay?" Frank asked in his usual composed voice.

"Yes, there was an incident, and some resulting damage, but everything is settled now. Would you like to come up?"

"Yes".

A knock vibrated through the main door to the suite seconds later. He had already been on his way up from his office and had called as a mere formality. I let him in, even though he had a key. I walked him to the damage. He assessed everything quietly then paused before asking what had happened. He knew us too well to assume that my brother and I had fought. So I decided with the truth

"Something invisible held me down in the bed, as its grip heated up like a stove burner. When Perseus came to help, it threw him to the wall and then the floor. It knocked me against the headboard and then it was gone just as quickly as it came."

"Did you see what did this to you?"

"It wasn't a person. Maybe it was a spirit? It claimed to want me."

"That is a given, Ms. Andromeda."

"In what way, Frank?" Perseus asked.

"In many ways, Mr. Perseus. It wanted Ms. Andromeda because it only affected the area she was in. That is, until you became involved in her rescue."

"I agree with that theory, but I'd like to know how this all happened."

"Did you get injured? I smell blood in the room." He looked at both of us.

"Yes, but it's already healed."

Frank came over and looked intensely at my neck. Then he backed away from me.

"Anything else that I should know about?"

I pulled my gown up to show him the burned skin on my ribcage.

"You do realize that few things can mark a vampire, correct?"

"Yes. Typically only another vampire can do so, since they have similar strengths."

"Correct. You also know there are things out there that we normally don't come across. But they still exist."

"Please, explain." I sat on the edge of the bed as I fought the urge to straighten the covers in Frank's presence.

"You and your brother have a power that is rare to humans and vampires alike."

"Yes, we have visions, mental communications and the ability to tap into each other with, or without, direct touch." We already knew this.

"Yes, but mentally talking to a vampire is not rare. Many can do it. But you received special powers as a human and it was passed down several generations. A vampire only gets it from a gifted maker."

"I didn't know that. Did you, Perseus?"

Perseus answered. "Yes, when I took some time to travel last year I lived with sisters that held a talent similar to ours. Now I see it was just a beginning to understand what was possible."

"I see. So, Frank, what you're saying is that black magic could be involved?"

"Exactly. I've met your voodoo priestess, Bambara, and know what magic she can do. You know she can tell you things that will frighten your immortal soul. She's a third generation, just as you are, but she has seen more in her lifetime than you have in yours. You've led a sheltered life for a gifted immortal. Even your brother has been to different covens and cultures, just to see what is out there. He can tell you stories, if he chooses to. I am older than you both and have seen enough to scare an immortal into indefinite hiding. However, you, Andromeda, have none of these experiences."

Frank walked over and put his hand under my chin. Looking deeply into his eyes I saw flashes of blood, carnage, and humans being raped and murdered while under a veil of black magic so thick that it choked me. He took his hand away, leaving my mind as my own. I knew Frank had done this on purpose, to prove his point. I hoped to never experience this type of tragedy in my life. My own past was mere sand to his beach of loss. Compared to that, I was humbled to have been so sheltered.

"I'm going to see Bambara today and I intend to ask her for help on the events that have been unfolding," I resolved.

Frank frowned. I knew he wanted the details of the other occurrences, so I briefly told him the story of the dream and the night in my bathtub.

"You need to tell all of this to Bambara. She'll need every little detail in order to help you fight this devious stalker. She has knowledge of things, and people, that are powerful enough to stop this and much worse. Have you met anyone recently that is suspicious?"

Then it hit me.

"We ran into someone from our past."

Perseus said, "You think he wants to finish what he didn't get to do long ago, don't you?"

"Anything is possible. The timing is perfect since this all started about the time he showed up."

Frank said, "See your priestess, I implore you, and be very careful. Something very dark is mixed into this. If this person can get to you using black magic, then your powers are not strong enough to keep you safely out of its reach."

With that, Frank said goodnight to us both. Perseus walked him out as I went to sleep on the empty side of my brother's king bed. I didn't want to be alone, in case my visitor decided to come back.

I got up after a few hours of fractured sleep before I finally gave up and joined Perseus at the breakfast table. He was pouring a glass of blood for each of us and I gladly took mine. We both knew that last night had sapped some of my usual stamina and it didn't hurt to have a little extra blood in the body to keep off the exhaustion.

My powers told me it was going to be the typical Southern muggy night, so I decided to dress for the weather in a halter dress that had a sunset printed on it. I pulled my hair up into a knot at the base of my neck and added my boots, since sandals or heels were a bad idea in the bayou. Throwing on my normal chunky jewelry, I met Perseus at the door so we could leave.

Bambara was a telepath as well as a third generation voodoo priestess. We'd both been born with our talents and our grandmothers had been our teachers to the trade. Bambara's grandmother had been able to talk to the dead, receive visions and see what ailed a person. It was an amazing thing to witness and many praised her talents. Unfortunately, there were just as many people who were terrified of her. She'd put enough fear in some people to keep them from ever going against her.

Haiti was Bambara's grandmother. I'd met her many years ago in a college Herbology class. I'd been by her side for the birth of her child Celeste, as well as when Celeste had given birth to Bambara, followed by Bambara having Claudette. They believed me to be good luck, so I was at every important day that the

women had. I loved them all and was even there when Haiti and
Celeste both passed away. Both women had held my hands as they
had let go of their bodies to travel into the spirit world. I'd wept
tears of blood.

We pulled onto the pitted gravel road that Bambara lived on as
dust churned around the car. I knew I'd have a layer of grime on
my skin by the time I headed back to the hotel.

Bambara didn't have air conditioning so she relied on open
windows and ceiling fans to cool off. The whole right side of her
house was dedicated to her craft, with only four rooms being
available to normal company.

Perseus parked the car at the end of the pier and called out a
greeting. I heard her call out to us from inside the open front door
so I walked up with a smile. She was sitting in her favorite chair
with her needlepoint and a pitcher of lemonade on the table beside
her. Everything in her house was antique but well maintained. I
loved her antique claw foot tub, which is where she'd been born.
Her couches were overstuffed velvet with dozens of handmade
pillows. No matter what the occasion was, the house was always
kept up and lemonade was already made. I hugged her but made
sure not to disturb her wicked looking needle. Perseus came up to
her and kissed her on the lips. He always lingered a bit when he
did that. She'd been much younger then and it had been many
years after Valentina's demise. My brother and Bambara had
carried on quite an affair. It had been short and had ended well
with them staying close friends. She had then started seeing a
priest in her area. She looked up at Perseus with a fire in her eyes
that belied her age. He sat down in the loveseat next to her chair
and grabbed a glass of cool lemonade, which, as she always did,
was already laced with herbs. I grabbed mine, took a big sip of the
refreshing liquid and got ready to tell her my story.

"Now child, tell me what's been going on."

"I've had some strange occurrences lately and feel that black
magic is involved. The timing lines up perfectly with a man from
my past showing up. He was the first mate to the man who'd
changed us. He was not a vampire at the time of my change but has
been changed since then. He's been following me lately and has

made a few appearances under the guise of being curious of how I've turned out."

"Do you believe he is the one causing your problems?"

"I'm not sure. It feels as if this is bigger than just one vampire but every time I attempt to trace the source I get a blinding headache. It's as if someone is protecting themselves from my sight."

Bambara paused for a minute, thinking. "You would be correct, child. This is bigger than one individual. Someone is touching you through dangerous magic and it is literally leaving a mark on you, is it not?"

"Yes. It marked me in a couple of different ways, one involving a small amount of blood. Black magic has to be involved for blocking my sight and it also has to be strong enough to cause physical pain without being present."

Again, Bambara paused before she spoke. "Also correct. There is black magic involved and it is indeed powerful. I can sense it. You've actually been bitten on two of these occasions and the burn is by the hand of the one channeling this power. No ordinary man can do these things. I also know that you have not completely healed from this, as you usually would."

"You where there last night, weren't you?"

I realized then that she'd been the one to break the connection of the black magic and had forced the invader to flee. The clue was the familiar air from last night coming from her patio. I also knew she was attuned to my needs. Who else could have been tied to me when I was defenseless? Perseus was amazed and had apparently not figured this out. This time Bambara actually looked up at me from her needlework and smiled.

"Yes child, I felt your pain and sent my spirit to defend you. The grip on you was strong but not too strong for me to dismiss. I was able to force him away, but not quickly enough to stop him from physically marking you."

"Thank you for your help. Bambara, does this mean that I may be permanently marked?"

She nodded. "I fear that he has marked you for his own and can trace that mark to wherever you are, at any time."

This unsettled Perseus. "Can we break this connection?"

"Yes and no. You have to find the person who's binding you and then find out what they're using to do it. It can be anything from a personal item to something made with black magic. Do you think this man from your past is the one holding the magic?"

I thought on it for a moment. I couldn't remember having any items that had gone missing, but some items were easier to come by. Jean Luc had been around my job and outside my home where it would've been child's play to get anything for a binding spell. A simple strand of my hair was something that was useful even in very basic spell casting.

"I'm not sure. I know that I don't get the same sinister presence when Jean Luc's present. Could he be able to protect his thoughts from me?"

"I see you're coming to the same conclusion I did. It is possible to bind you plus keep you at a distance at the same time. It's ancient magic and takes a great amount of power to do this. If this man doesn't seem to be a threat then he has someone powerful behind him."

"How far can he take this bind?"

"He can come to you at anytime, whether it's in person or in spirit. It'll tax him physically and mentally, but vampires heal quickly enough to accomplish this task. You need to get close enough to this person and get something personal of theirs. We may be able to use this object to reverse the magic. If you find something, bring it to me and I'll see what I can do. I can help you to protect yourself now, but it'll only cover so much."

She put down her needlework and motioned for me to follow her to the back of the house. I followed her into a small work area just before the back patio and stepped inside before she softly closed the door. She rummaged around for a few different things on the cluttered white shelves and placed them into my hands. She clasped her worn fingers around my full ones as she began to chant. The lights flickered for a moment. A shiver crawled down my spine. I closed my eyes and repeated after her until the lights stabilized.

Patting my closed hands she said to me, "Keep one of these on you at all times, even in the tub. He can still get to you, but he'll not be able to do as much damage. I wish I could reverse this mark but black magic is out of my everyday range. I could do it, but I swore to my mother that I wouldn't use black magic unless it was life or death. Find out what you can about this man because I fear this is only the beginning."

She looked at me and I saw the sorrow in her old eyes.

"Did you see something happen to me?"

"I know only what this black magic can do. I see great sadness and misfortune for you. I knew that I had to help you last night. You and your brother are bound to me because of my mother and her mother before her, so anything this powerful will come through me as it does you."

She lifted up her peasant blouse and I saw a faint pink mark on her stomach, identical to my own. She yanked it back down and grabbed my hand again.

"Andromeda, I drank your blood just like my ancestors and I will always be with you. A blood bond can break, but not one that is owned by the spirit. I've seen what you've seen and I see what is ahead of us. This dreadful beast has you marked and I fear he won't stop until he fully possesses you. Use the gift your ancestors gave you and never go back on your faith. If you want this man, this Justin, then take warning that it bodes ill for you. If you choose to fight, then you'll do so to the extent of your being. I'll watch over you. I have something for Perseus as well. I'll give it to him at dinner."

"Thank you. I'll get back to you when I have more information. I'll leave you two to your dinner and leave my issues at the door when you go. I hope that you have a most enjoyable evening."

I kissed her weathered cheek and let myself out of the room before I headed back to Perseus. I made Perseus promise to let my situation go as he took Bambara out to dinner. Bambara felt that nothing would happen in the next few hours due to the amount of strength it had taken to mark me last night. Perseus was relieved as he released me, took Bambara's hand, and left with her.

I took my time around the bayou once they were gone and I meandered toward the old cemetery. I'd found my way here on more than one occasion, and I sat, as always, on an old weathered stone bench by Haiti's grave. It was then I looked over what Bambara had given me.

There was a leather strand with a wax sealed seashell hanging from it, and a leather pouch that was tied shut, but once opened I found a tiny vial with ground up items inside. I slipped the necklace around my neck and placed the other two items in my pockets. I felt another shiver dance across my skin as the necklace touched my bare skin. Wind went through the trees as I heard a chant way off in the distance. At that very moment Perseus was receiving his own charm and it was also tied to me. I whispered another thank you into the wind and got up to find my way back to the hotel.

As I walked, I checked in with everyone. Danya was at work with a steady crowd. Justin was walking the dark streets, in deep thought. Perseus was walking out of the house with Bambara. She was smiling as he settled her into the Porsche. She had changed and was looking forward to her night, even with the car top down. He handed her the silk scarf from his pocket and waited until she had tied it around her hair before he took off down her gravel driveway. I shut off the connection so they'd have privacy for the night.

A couple of hours before daylight, I went back to the hotel and felt refreshed after my commune with nature. I'd found a note left by Frank on the breakfast table.

He had written, "There will be a knock on your door five minutes after you arrive in for the evening. I was told by Ms. Bambara that you would need a little something extra this evening and to see to it for her. It will be one of my girls. She has ingested a potion that your brother dropped off on his way out. He informed me that there are to be no interruptions in your evening. If you do not want this visitor then do not answer the door and she will not disturb you again. This is your choice. Sleep well."

I wondered about this arrangement that had been set up for me. I knew I only had two minutes before someone would be at the door. I was to drink from this woman and that bothered me, since I usually didn't feed this way. I would only do this because of Bambara. I trusted her with my life.

Chapter Six

A knock came to the door just at five minutes. I sighed as I went to answer it. I opened the door to see a woman about twenty-five years old with waist length blonde hair wearing a turquoise halter dress. She looked like a beautiful mermaid. I waved for her to come in. She stood inside the door as I locked it back up. She never took those eyes off of me.

"Where would you like me?" She asked.

It was as if this was normal for her. I was never too old to be surprised.

"What instructions were you given?"

She smiled. "I was available for a couple of hours, so I was handed something to drink and was instructed to come to your room."

"Were you told why?" I asked before walking toward her.

"Yes, I'm aware of what you are and that this isn't your normal practice. I'm not afraid nor have I been compelled. I trust Frank and he trusted what was to be given to me."

"Okay, since you know what is expected of you, then I'll give you the choice of how this will happen and where you would be more comfortable having this done."

She looked around the room and asked where my room was. I pointed her in that direction. She walked into my room. I followed a few paces behind her and saw her lean against my mattress. She ran her hand over the covers and turned back to me.

"I have somewhere to be tonight and wasn't expecting to see a vampire so I may not be dressed appropriately." She said as she indicated the straps of her own halter dress.

I understood what she meant.

"So, you don't want marks on your neck or shoulders."

This was getting more and more interesting.

She laughed. "Yes, so that leaves any other area that would be covered by my dress."

"My saliva would close the wound up but it'd still be tender to the touch."

"They told me you were very considerate. I'm glad they were correct."

She held out her hand for me. I came over but ignored her outstretched hand as I sat next to her on the edge of the bed.

"I'm glad you're comfortable with this, because I'm not."

She squeezed my hand as it lay in my lap. "If you can actually heal up the wound, then you can choose the area that you'd like to bite."

"The wrist would hurt less."

She whispered, "Go on".

I motioned for her to lie down on the bed and told her to relax. I held her delicate wrist in my hands and shut out any other thoughts in my head. I didn't want this to be a bad experience for her and knew that most had even gotten a sexual rush from the act itself. I also wanted to shut out the voice that told me this was crossing a delicate line with my more human morals. This was a willing woman and I had to do as Bambara had instructed. She wouldn't steer me wrong. I hesitantly bit into her soft flesh, just below her palm. She gasped. Her blood was strong and full of herb essence. It was heady and intoxicating. It was the best blood that I'd ever tasted.

There was a warm flush that flowed through my body. She moaned as the sexual side effects took over her senses. There was no more pain for her. Only feeling. Her eyes dilated. Her breath rasped unevenly. I couldn't say that I was as affected as she was, but I wasn't too far off. I could feel her strength as it seeped into my body, so I slowly withdrew from her. I made sure to run my tingling tongue over the small puncture wounds and saw them close up quickly. Her breath hitched at my ministrations. I slowly stepped outside of the bedroom and leaned my reeling head against the doorframe.

I became super sensitive with that tainted blood as it pumped through my veins. Everything became brighter, more defined. I'd been told that this was the closet I would ever feel to being drunk off power and alcohol. I stayed still for a few moments and absorbed the wonderful feeling as I waited for my guest to come out. She hid her face as she stumbled past me and into the foyer.

"Were you compensated for your trouble?" I asked, not wanting to insult her.

"Um, yes," she said without looking at me.

"I appreciate you doing this for me. I hope I didn't hurt you."

She looked at me this time, then walked up to me.

"I'll be honest by saying that it was an unexpected pleasure and I'm glad that I could help you. I've never experienced that before and I'd do this for you again, any time you needed."

"Oh."

"If you ever need me again, please have Frank call me. I would be more than happy to take care of your needs."

I knew she meant more than the service she'd provided tonight and I was indeed flattered. I'd never had a woman show her attraction for me, on any level. It was embarrassing but also very liberating. I smiled and thanked her before walking her to the door. After locking up, I called Frank to thank him as well.

"Anytime, madam. Her name is Angelica and I hope she was satisfactory."

I could feel his amusement over my awkward situation.

"She was more than adequate. She even thanked me for the experience."

"Ah, I see. I had thought to send you one of my drivers but he didn't have the strength for the task at hand. I had hoped not to offend you by sending one of my ladies up."

"It was strange but not offensive. She offered her services again, at any time."

"Well, as long as you are satisfied." He insinuated much with his comment.

"Not quite in that way, but it's a thought for the future. My sexual status has still not changed."

That was putting it politely.

"I see. Well, let me know if you have any other needs that can be taken care of. Sleep well."

He hung up and I shook my head as I got ready for bed.

I walked into the bedroom where her scent owned the very air, as my sensitive nose inhaled deeply. I took my bath and then slipped into the still scented sheets as I dreamed peacefully.

* * * *

Sunday, I woke to my brother humming away at the small dinning room table between our rooms. I slipped on my robe and walked outside to see what he'd planned for our evening. He had building plans in front of him and was all smiles. I pinched his arm, too roughly, as I went to sit beside him. That brought his head up from his beloved papers.

"You seem very happy this morning. I guess that you had a wonderful evening?" I smiled at him.

"You'd be guessing right. We had a wonderful dinner followed by strenuous dancing. That woman may be older but she can keep up with any lady younger than her," he said as he pinched me back. "Speaking of which, how was your night?"

"Someone has been telling stories out of class."

He shrugged, as he kept his mischievous smile. "Bambara talked to Frank in front of me and I saw the young lady in question. I wondered how the situation would turn out. You were sending off some peculiar vibes last night. Do you mind killing my curiosity?"

"It was an experience that I will not soon forget. She was a beautiful woman and she loved what happened."

"One of these days we'll have to end that out of date virgin status and welcome you into the world of sexual delight. Maybe we can get someone to take care of that while we're in town. I'm sure Frank knows of someone who can teach you a few things?"

"Now is not the time, but I do appreciate the thought. When I'm ready for sex, I'll take care of it myself." I got up from the table.

His roar of laughter filled the room at my double entendre faux pas but I ignored him. I felt exhilarated about this evening and the opening of the new place and wasn't going to let him tease me out of my good mood. I still had mixed emotions about the whole experience of sex but had decided to just let it go after I'd woken up with the feeling of invincibility.

I curled up on the butter soft leather couch with a cup of blood-laced Turkish coffee and listened to Perseus talk about the plans he had for the evening. We'd woken a little earlier in the evening than normal so we could meet the real estate agent at the property. The agent was human and wasn't asking questions about the oddly late time of the appointment considering how much he'd get paid for his time if the deal went through. I finished my coffee, dressed in lightning speed, and was at the door within five minutes.

"I guess your night left you with a little pep in your step, hmm?"

He let us out of the room and down to the already waiting car.

"You could say that. I feel like I could stay up for days and still have my skin tingle with the electricity in the air."

I jumped over the rolled down window and into the convertible's smooth seats. I felt like a kid again and the blood-laced coffee only amplified it. He shook his head at me, slid on his sunglasses and spun the Porsche out of the parking lot. All I could do was hold on and giggle like a schoolgirl. We sped toward town and pulled onto Hwy 10 with no traffic.

I leaned back into the plush leather and listened to the hum of the world around me. I felt so sexy it was laughable. I still felt Angelica in my blood and wondered what she was doing at that moment. That simple thought tuned me right in on her as she had dinner with another client.

She felt the connection, which was rare for a human. Her head was bending over her glass of champagne. She smiled into the glass. The gentleman's cell phone went off at that time and he excused himself. She was glad he was distracted because she didn't want him to hear her whisper my name. She went over the feelings she had gotten from the bite I had given her and it turned her on. I quickly closed the contact between us as her client came back but I still felt her near me. It was amazing. It was as if I'd been sitting next to her the whole time. Her blood buzzed like a bee inside my body. I laughed again and looked over at my brother to see his dark gaze already on my face.

He stopped the car at a red light. I saw tension in his expression. I was seeing too much of that with him lately. He pulled into the parking lot of a three-story glass front building. The sky was open around the building, a perfect vantage point for looking at the stars. I liked it right away and saw the possibilities.

I reached for the door handle but was stopped when Perseus grabbed my hand.

"What happened a few minutes ago?" He asked with a frown on his face.

"What do you mean? I was just looking at the property and wondered how it looks inside." I leaned back in the seat, confused.

He leaned back and looked at his watch. "We're twenty-five minutes early, so spill it."

"What do I need to spill?" I heard the crickets around us and waited for his answer. "Wait a minute, are you trying to get more information out of me about last night? I thought we were past that?"

He shook his beautiful head, closed his eyes, and sighed. "No, what just happened before we pulled into here? You can sit there and act as if nothing happened but I won't believe you."

Then it hit me.

"Did you see Angelica?"

He opened his eyes and they were dark with passion. "Oh boy,"

Questions ran through my mind. How much did he see? Had he seen it like I had? How did he feel about this? But before I could voice any of these concerns, he answered them all in order.

"All of it. No, it was like I was watching the two of you. Weird."

Oh shit.

"Ya think?"

"Wait, I haven't said anything. What the hell?"

"I was wondering what side effects you'd have and now I know."

"What side effects? Do you mean that you knew something would happen to me for drinking from Angelica?"

Shit.

"I agree."

He heard every little word as if I was shouting at him. I concentrated on building a mental block but was sidetracked as he reached over and tapped my nose with his fingertip.

"Honey, it's okay. Bambara told me the potion would enhance your powers plus a few you didn't know you had. We weren't sure how far it'd push you but it was necessary for us to try to protect you. I'm sorry if this is too much to deal with. I'll try to keep a distance between us while you work this out. I only warned you because it took affect faster than we'd imagined. Don't be ashamed and don't push me out. I can help you through this. Bambara left five other vials and you're to drink them in the same way, once a week, to hold back who ever is trying to get to you. We'll have to see how fast you burn it off before we give you the second dose. She told me not to say anything but to watch you closely for the first day. I'm sorry, but I had to do something to protect you."

I sighed. "It's okay. I understand why you guys did it, so I'm not mad. I wish I'd been warned before hand, but I guess you didn't want to worry me further."

He nodded. "So, if you have any really weird things that happen, or start to feel strange, please tell me."

I laughed so hard at this that tears gathered in my eyes.

When I finally stopped I looked at him and said, "Pers, my body is humming. I have some black magic vampire after me. I'm sexually attracted to a human woman. What is non-strange about all of that?"

He laughed as well and I embraced that laughter while I had it.

I leaned my head onto his shoulder. "What other things do I need to worry about?"

He kissed the top of my head. "Andy, just take care of your self. I need you to be aware of things while we unfold this mystery. You have to tell me if you feel anything other than what you're feeling now. Don't be surprised if it gets bizarre."

I didn't have much time to digest this as a new model Mercedes pulled in beside us. I got out of the car and shut the door just as a gust of wind blew my skirt up to my hips. I didn't care and just brushed it back down as I walked away from the car.

Then I heard it, the thoughts coming from the real estate agent. I turned around and caught the brunette man as he ogled my butt. He had wished that my skirt had gone up higher. I looked at him until he looked me in the eyes. He was embarrassed that I'd caught him in the act.

I turned on my heel and caught up with Perseus as he walked up the steps to the front door of the building. The agent jogged past us to unlock the door as we got there. I heard him thinking about my legs. This new power could be sinfully fun. I wondered what else I could do.

After a quick perusal of the floor plan, I ran over and hugged Perseus around his neck. The place was wonderful, so I whispered that he should buy it. He smiled and swung me around like I was a little girl again. I laughed and heard the agent's thoughts again. I whispered into Perseus' ear that I could hear the other man's thoughts and that he was checking out my thighs. I laughed as the agent wondered about my relationship with Perseus and I relayed this to Perseus as well. I was a little kid in a sparkly new candy store.

I winked at the agent. "Well, sweetie, I like it but my brother needs to haggle over a few issues."

The agent grinned as he mentally calculated how much he could make off of the deal. I turned my back on them both as I headed back down to the first floor.

The guys shook hands on a price that was a few thousand under the original asking price. As the agent walked us out, I swatted his butt. It brought a lovely flush to his skin and raised his heart rate to a frantic rush that made my mouth water. He then locked up and I walked to Perseus' car as my brother laughed at my antics.

"This new you is delightfully crazy. What am I going to do with you? Are you going to be like this for the next month?" Perseus asked as he turned onto the service road.

"I'm not sure, but this could be a lot of fun."

I loved all of this and wondered what more I could expect from the next few weeks. I wasn't afraid as I looked forward to these intriguing side effects.

* * * *

Perseus had everything arranged after that, so we headed back to the hotel to pack up for home. The task didn't take long, and I handed the key over to the lady at the front desk in no time at all and walked up to Frank's office door not wanting to be rude and leave without saying goodbye, especially after our little escapade.

As I went to knock, the door opened and Angelica came out. I could tell she'd been crying and was surprised to see me standing there. Wiping her face with the back of her hand, she whispered a greeting to me. Frank glanced my way and motioned me inside but I stopped Angelica before I entered the doorway.

I softly asked Frank, "What happened?"

"A client was rough with Angelica and I am on my way to deal with the gentleman."

I looked Frank in the eyes and smiled. He nodded. He knew I'd handle this for him and in my own discreet way. I turned and saw Perseus standing behind Angelica just outside of the doorway. I told him I'd meet him back in the lobby in about fifteen minutes.

My taking care of this solved a few problems. Frank wouldn't have to crease his immaculate Armani suit, and I'd get in a quick feeding before the drive home, plus I'd repay my debt to Angelica for her kindness.

I grabbed her hand and laced my fingers with hers. Reaching over, I wiped away the tears and asked her to take me to the client's room. She hesitated, knowing what I was, but I made the decision for her as I closed my eyes and concentrated. I saw the violator in his room on the fourth floor. He was pencil thin and resembled a slimy bookworm, bottle thick black-rimmed eyeglasses and all. He'd pinned her to the bed and had slapped her around before she'd wrenched away for her escape.

I opened my eyes before I slipped off the scarf she'd sloppily tied around her shoulders and saw bruises beginning to form. I looked down at the small circular marks on her ankles. There was the evidence of the travesty done to her. I saw fear in her eyes and it pained me to see that on her beautiful face. I saw that same pain in Danya's eyes as I'd noticed the scar across her ribcage. I took care of the people who where there for me, and Angelica was now included in that special list.

"No more tears."

She bit her lip and nodded. I pulled her toward the empty elevator. I knew what room he was in and felt the tension build in Angelica as she pondered at my level of power. She'd only had brief moments with vampires, but I was an exception.

I knocked on his door and willed him to open it. He had a towel wrapped around his neck and his glasses were missing. A quick read of his mind told me that without his glasses, he didn't recognize Angelica.

"Two more girls. He must have sent me some fresh meat since the last one was such a dud."

I laughed dryly before navigating Angelica to the foot of the bed. It was still rumpled from his earlier attempt to rape her. I felt Angelica shudder at the thought of what could have happened but she bravely composed herself, knowing she'd be leaving in a different manner this time.

"Don't you wear glasses?" I asked him, as he wiped the shaving cream from his chin.

"Yes, I do. Why do you ask?"

"Put them on, please."

He shrugged and grabbed them off of the nightstand. Then he recognized her. "You! Why the hell are you back up here? You're not woman enough for me. Didn't you hear me say that before?"

He tossed the towel at her but I intercepted it in mid air. I took it from there.

"Sir, you were rude to my friend. I think you owe her an apology."

I twisted the towel around both hands as I gave him a moment to compose himself. He laughed, a bad decision on his part. I was on him in a second and wrapped the towel around his thin neck.

"I didn't hear that apology. Would you like to try that again?"

I squeezed a little harder. He gagged. I slapped his shoulder, identical to how he'd struck Angelica. He cried out. I covered his mouth just as the sound came out and whispered into his ear.

"I'm still waiting."

He still wouldn't say the words, even under duress. I slipped my hand away from his mouth. He wasted the breath to curse me. I smiled. He wasn't going to apologize. This was going to get interesting.

"You bitch! Why the hell would I apologize to this piece of trash? She's nobody and not worth the time I wasted on trying to fuck her ass!"

"Tsk, tsk, tsk. Bad move, Bennie."

He was shocked that I knew his nickname. I saw that his job as a traveling salesman had allowed him to do this to several women of the working class. Angelica wasn't the first, by any means, but she was the luckiest, and certainly the last. This habit would end tonight.

Chapter Seven

He was still cursing when I shoved him to the floor. I'd hoped in vain that he'd at least act as if he was remorseful, but he was a true menace. Remorse was not in his nature. I crawled on top of him as Angelica stood close by. My fingernails grew into razor blades and I raked them down Bennie's throat. Red beads welled up. I breathed in the heady scent of fresh blood and his fear. He yelped as I ran the tip of my tongue over the largest bead on his throat.

Angelica sat before me and I placed her hands on each side of his mouth so she could muffle his screams at any time. I looked into her eyes as I waited for her acceptance. She nodded. I knew then she was okay with what ever I was about to do to her attacker. Without a second thought, I pressed my lips firmly against her parted ones. Bennie squirmed beneath us, getting my full attention. I pulled away and focused back on Bennie.

"You freaky bitch! Either fuck me or get the hell off of me. And don't even think about getting paid for this."

"Oh Bennie, it's going to cost you, all right. The price I demand is your blood, the one thing that keeps this miserable excuse of a body alive. You are the pathetic, worthless one and you're going to be taught a lesson tonight."

"Just take my wallet and get out, you freak."

She covered his mouth again.

I concentrated on his beady eyes.

"Listen to me, Bennie. You are never going to hurt another woman as long as you live."

His eyes dilated. His breathing slowed. I had him. He was an easier prey than all the women he'd abused over the last few years. I looked at Angelica one last time before completing my task and saw the excitement in her wide, blue eyes. Bennie struggled again, seeing I was distracted. He was wrong again. I stared back into his eyes and felt the thread of his weak soul.

In a low monotone voice I said, "Bennie, you are sorry for what you have done."

He nodded.

"You will never do this again. You won't remember what happened with us, but you will remember my words. Anytime you even attempt to abuse another woman, you'll feel nothing but pain and fear. Do you understand me?"

Again, he nodded. I took that moment to sink my sharp teeth into his trembling flesh and drank. His scream was silenced as Angelica moved in to cover his gaping lips. I put my full weight on him and cut off his air. I didn't care about any of it and kept drinking. Just as I started to break contact, I instilled fear into him of a punishing sort. This would ensure the safety of any woman who crossed his path. By then he was on the verge of passing out, so I reluctantly withdrew. I licked his limp neck and the blood clotted. There was no fight left anymore in Bennie the abuser. This would be the last that anyone would see of that character. I licked the trace of blood from my lips as Angelica released him.

I reached out to her and we got up. She gave one last look to the man who had attacked her, and then she looked at me. I saw her relief and gratitude. I held her hand as I walked her back to the elevator, leaving the incident behind us. I'd need to let Frank know how I'd left things and make sure Angelica was okay before I left.

"Angelica, don't give his words power. You know who you are and where you need to be. Choose where you want to go from here and never look back. Take this as a lesson learned."

She squeezed my hand as we exited the elevator. She needed to take some time to figure out where to go from here, but I already knew that she'd decided to leave her current profession.

Frank's door was open, so we went up to his desk. I gave him enough information to know that there would be no need to clean up after my actions. Bennie wouldn't be making this mistake again and was lucky to have any life at all. Frank nodded his approval and added that Bennie would not be welcome back, though it made little difference since I had compelled him.

"Ms. Angelica, I take it you have had a change of heart with your current position in life?" Frank asked as he sensed her emotional state.

She nodded and cleared her voice. "Yes sir. I believe I need to think about where my life is headed and do something better with the time I have left."

I squeezed the hand that I was still holding and nodded at Frank.

"Well, take a few days to think things over and let me know what you have decided. You will still have a place here, if you need it." He waved a dismissal at her.

We both knew he had a generous spirit, which he kept hidden. I let go of her hand as she headed out his door and heard Perseus talk to her as he waited for me. I sent him a small image of what had happened to her and to Bennie. He knew enough from those images to take a much needed step toward a fresh start for her. I smiled and brought my attention back to Frank.

"Well, I will not say goodbye, since I know you will be back very soon. You have gotten another ally during your trip, not that I am surprised." He lowered his voice to a mere whisper and asked, with a smile, "Will she be your consort?"

"No. She has a path to choose and I won't stop her from making her own way."

"You could easily have this mortal. I believe she would love you for it." He poured himself a cup of blood-laced tea.

"You may be correct. But I am who I am and that's not how I live my life. My life was violently changed and I wasn't given a chance. She won't be like me. She's now on the right path and will keep her free will for as long as she lives."

"I admire you, Ms. Andromeda. You have so much passion and love. Beings of our world crush humans at the slightest provocation without worry or guilt, but not you. You are truly one of a kind. I am thankful to live an eternity knowing you. Now, grab your dear brother and head home before the sun sees you first."

"Thank you, Frank. I'll see you soon. I believe I'll be seeing my new ally as well. She already has a new job lined up and only needs to make the first move."

I saw an image of Angelica shaking my brother's hand as she walked off to start her new life. She had plans to make and had her first sight of real hope in years. I showed Frank my new image of her at Medusa's Manor and he nodded again at my vision of Angelica's future.

"She seems to be an asset already. I wish you both peace in the coming days."

I wished him a good night and headed out into the parking lot where the Porsche waited. Once at the car, Perseus informed me of his talk with Angelica. I wasn't rude enough to tell him that I already knew what had been decided. I smiled and agreed with him.

"She certainly made an impression," he admitted as he thought over all the things that had happened this weekend.

He wasn't even aware of the things I had experienced, nor was I going to fill him in on all of it.

My little sidetrack cost us some valuable time and dawn was quickly approaching the closer we got to Savannah. I normally felt sleep creep into my system this close to dawn, but instead I felt invigorated. I felt as if I could stay up indefinitely, just to see if I could do it under these circumstances. But I decided not to tempt fate, this time.

* * * *

I woke, but stayed snuggled in my soft sheets. I heard Perseus as he hummed while he signed papers. I sensed that he had slept restlessly and had been mostly focused on his list of tasks to be completed during the night.

My thoughts went to Angelica and I saw her in her room with a list of open apartments in New Orleans. She was looking for something in a decent budget range and knew she had so few items to take that only her luggage and a few boxes were necessary. I scanned the pages with mid blowing speed and brought her attention to the last page where a furnished loft apartment would be ready in a week's time. She would have a couple of days to close up at Frank's and then a day to travel to her new home.

It was in a quiet neighborhood with a recreation center and small park right outside her building. I closed our connection before she realized that it was me guiding her to a safe place to live.

I got up and took a quick shower before meeting Perseus in the dining room. He was on the phone and I waved as I headed out the door for work. I took a deep breath and inhaled the scents around me. Being a vampire made me sensitive to every feeling and emotion but after the herbs I had ingested it became even more so. I could taste the salt in the air that came from the ocean. It exhilarated me. I hummed as I strolled to work and thought of the coming few weeks as Medusa's Manor was being prepared for its grand opening. Perseus would have a full schedule, which meant the house would be quiet again. But despite that, and despite this evil presence, I didn't worry about being home alone. I felt sorry for anyone who dared to break into my home. They wouldn't leave intact.

As I got closer to work, I could smell Danya's perfume in the air. She had shown up to work an hour early. I walked into the back door and was behind her as she turned to see me standing inches from her. She gave a shriek, and I caught the bottle she was holding as it slipped from her grasp. I put it down before she realized the speed I had used. I needed to be more aware of my actions while the herbs where in my system.

"Sorry, I didn't mean to scare you. You were so absorbed that you didn't hear me come in."

She waved at my comment and fired off questions. "How was your trip? What did the place look like? Where is your brother? Did he buy it?"

"Okay, in order. Interesting, perfect for a new place, at home for a few more minutes and yes."

"So, that means the place will open soon and he'll be super focused on it for the next few weeks. How big is it and what's it like?"

I told her the layout and that Perseus had already hired his first employee for the club.

This surprised her since we usually went through staffing agencies for new locations. "Well, he must have impressed you guys."

"He is a she and yes, you can say that she did. We met her at the hotel since she worked there until the day we left. She's relocating." I could feel the tension building in Danya as I gave her this information.

"Huh, a lady. Is she a waitress?"

She was trying to find out if she needed to be jealous of Angelica. Wait until she saw the blonde bombshell in person.

"No, I believe he hired her to start as the hostess. I warmed up to her right from the start."

Understatement.

"Oh, okay then."

"So, how was your weekend?"

"I got my nails done and met a guy."

"Is he cute?"

"Yeah, he is. He came in and talked to me for a while and then asked for my number before he left. We've texted a few times since then. Besides, I can't wait around forever for Mr. Right."

She didn't offer any other information and she was right about waiting on my stubborn brother. I dropped the subject all together and got to work. I hoped that things ended better for Justin and me. I wanted to be with him but I had to stand back so he could make a clear decision.

Later on, Danya asked more questions about the building and when opening night was scheduled. I gave more details and we discussed ideas for the décor. She loved the mythology theme that we stuck with but we never explained our background with it. Sometimes, it still hurt to think of the Greek and Roman mythology that had fascinated my mother. It was the books she had learned to read with and had taught us by those same worn pages.

Frank had called Perseus with a list of potential employees and it looked good so far; the current job market had left many people looking for good paying jobs.

Of course, Danya and I would be there opening night to help fill in any gaps. She kept a cool head, like Perseus, and that was always an advantage. I wanted to dress the girls in togas for opening night, just to see how Danya would take it. And upon further thought, I decided that Angelica would look fabulous in one as hostess. Maybe we could make short ones for the waitresses. I sent the image to Perseus and felt him smile. He loved looking at women, and short, sexy togas would fit the bill plus look amazing.

Danya's phone went off halfway through the slow night so she was able to take it. I knew it was her new guy friend and he wanted to come by the bar for a couple of hours.

Perseus came in and waved at us over his phone, then shut himself in his office to go over the papers he had brought in. New employees would be tough to hire when the building wasn't even ready for business and we only worked at night. I heard him take a phone call from Frank on ladies who wanted to work for us that previously had been in Frank's employ but wanted a different way of life, like Angelica. She had told a couple of them to see if it would work out and all of them had promised not to bring there former job into this new one. We would take their word for it and go from there.

I wasn't having very many customers as well, so I decided to help the rest of the staff for the remainder of the night. While I closed up my table, I saw a stocky man with curly brown hair come in and motion to Danya. She smiled at him and waved him over to the bar. I smelled the ocean on him and thought that maybe he was staying on Tybee Island. She hugged him over the bar and had him sit down. The look on her face showed how happy she was that he had shown up.

I went to bus some tables and noticed her run by with some chicken wings as I took dishes to the sink. The kitchen had already closed down so she must have warmed them up for her friend. I started sweeping the floors in the far corner and saw him pass me as he headed to the restroom. He looked at me twice, and then hurried by. Danya waved me over so I set the broom down for the time being.

"My friend came in to see me, did you see him?"

"Yes, he passed me a moment ago. He's cute and looks Latin, what's his name?"

"Thomãs and yes, his parents are from Argentina. He's in town for a few weeks doing some work for his boss."

"Ah."

"It's a shame he's not a local guy. That means he's just here temporarily. But I'm going to try to have some fun. Here he comes," she smiled as he came around the corner.

He sat down and I saw a strange look cross his features. Did I make him nervous? He gave me a weak smile before he finished off his beer.

"Thomãs, this is my best friend Andromeda. Andromeda, meet Thomãs. He came in over this weekend and we kind of hit it off."

I reached out my hand but he only looked at it over his empty glass and then nodded at me.

"Hello." I withdrew my hand and nodded back at him.

I reached over to get his empty plate and glass and he shrank away from me. If I hadn't seen him hug Danya, then I would've wondered if he had a phobia about being touched.

"Hey, I have a wonderful idea," Danya said quickly. "Thomãs works for an antique dealer and we just happen to need items for the new location we are setting up. What do you say we look at some?"

I thought about it. "Yes, that's a wonderful idea. Thomãs, what kind of items do you carry?"

"We're currently bringing items over to some stores on River Street and we do a little bit of everything," he said, without looking at my face. "The boss handles small pieces that would complete a set or one of kind pieces that collectors are looking for."

"All our places carry a theme and what we need are things that would go great with mythology. Right now I think it would be great to find some old frames or a trunk that have a Greek feel to them. Anything with snakes would work as well."

"I saw a trunk that had snakes carved into the brass fittings. Would that do?" He offered as he toyed with Danya's fingers. He still wouldn't look at me.

"Yes, that would work nicely in the sitting area on the second floor, depending on how big it is."

"It's about three feet in length, four feet wide, and two feet tall. I may also have some picture frames that would work. I'll look through everything after I leave here."

"Thank you, that'd be great."

"I'll bring the trunk by so that you guys can check it out." He got out his wallet to pay Danya for his bill.

"You can do that?"

He shrugged as he watched Danya. "Yeah, I deliver everything for him, so it's no big deal for me to take a piece to someone. The boss knows I'll do what he tells me to, so no harm in trying to get a sale."

I murmured my okay and told Danya to get the info on when it could be brought by. She was going to talk to Perseus about it before she left, to make sure he had time to see the piece as well. I went back to cleaning up, and had very little left to do when the bar actually closed.

After seeing the final customer out the door, I walked out the back door and saw Danya as she walked away with Thomãs. I didn't bother to say goodnight and just headed home. Several things were nagging at me and one of them was how peculiar Thomãs had acted around me. I began to replay the night but got distracted when Perseus came up behind me.

He had gotten a lot of work accomplished and wanted to go over all of it with me before I went to sleep. He was talking so low and fast that the normal person would have thought that he was mumbling. But I was used to it, and I caught all of the details he explained.

I felt like we were being watched as we got closer to home but Perseus was too distracted to notice. He loved being this involved in something. He had been amazing as a human but was extraordinary as a vampire. I didn't bother to tell Perseus that he was ignoring a possible threat, since I wasn't getting a negative vibe or any ominous visions from our stalker. I stuck with my gut, keeping my mouth shut and my mind open.

I continued to keep up the conversation as I mentally watched out for our stalker. We got to the house and I felt a gust of wind as we reached the front porch, thus proving I was right not to worry. Whoever it was had run away before we could see who it was and I couldn't catch any scents in the air.

****

The next night I felt something new—need. It wasn't my own, even though I did need some warm blood, and I sat in the middle of my bed and concentrated on this new emotion. I quickly realized it was Justin's emotion, and he was thinking about me. He had been trying to rationalize his strong feelings for me and had come to a decision. He wanted me and could care less what the future held, as long as I was in it. He had planned to come to the bar tonight to tell me his decision. I would accept his answer.

I knew we were meant to be together. Though I had nothing to back it up, I just knew, deep down. But I would have to tell him the truth about myself to see if there was any future to look forward to. I could feel he was reliving the electric kiss we had shared, and he wondered if it would always be that intense. It scared him, but he wasn't going to chicken out on something so powerful.

As I thought about what I had felt with that kiss I unconsciously linked with him, as I had with Angelica. He looked up, as if I had come into his room. I saw those gorgeous eyes and the raw need inside of them. He wanted to be with me badly and we both knew it. He whispered my name and instantly knew I could hear him. He questioned this and I whispered for him not to worry about it. I sent a wave of calm feelings over our connection to make this less of a shock to him. We kept talking in our minds and he seemed considerably calmer with this new piece of knowledge about my powers.

"Yes, this is part of my power, but I'm experiencing a side effect from some of it."

He frowned. "You said there were special things about you and you weren't joking. This is going to take a minute to get used to.

I explained. "With me, you always need to keep an open mind. I have an annoying little stalker who isn't a threat but I enlisted a spell, of sorts, to give me added protection just in case. I assure you that there's no need to worry, because Perseus is watching over me like a big brother should."

"I'm still bothered, but I'll let it go if you promise to take care of yourself. Besides, I don't know you well enough yet to get all bossy and protective on you."

"Justin, there are many things we need to learn about each other. And we can start on that tonight. If anything, I think you'll be more freaked out by the real me than by any trick we can do."

He shook his head. "I can't make any promises. Only time will tell."

Questions ran through his head and I laughed at how many of them he could think of in such a short time. Him being a full-blooded male, it was not surprising that he was already thinking of sex with me. Men. I answered what I could, with as little information as possible. I didn't think I'd ever be bored with Justin. The boldness that I was experiencing from the potion had me responding a little outside my normal behavior. "Crazy sex for us? Fireworks are putting it mildly. Per my visions, we'd light up the sky better than any Fourth of July ever planned."

He was surprised by my statement, so I sent him the image of us in my bed again and his eyes got dark with need.

All I could say was, "Me, too".

He got a mischievous look on his face and closed his eyes. He was imagining me, to see if he could pull off another side of the trick. And he wasn't too far off on his perception of my body, clever man. He ran his hand over my face and stopped at my lips, caressed them. I could feel him as he trailed that hand down my sensitive neck, down to cup my left breast. In his mind, it was soft and perky. In reality, it was harder than he imaged, in more ways than one. My nipples got tight and I inhaled. I could almost smell him next to me. He concentrated harder and blew air over the nipple. It ached.

His hand dipped lower to trace imaginary designs over my belly. I moaned softly as he dipped his hand between my legs. It felt like he was running his fingers over me. I couldn't help but feel lost. I had never experienced this before. How should I react? I was a four hundred year old virgin. He whispered for me to relax.

I was still sitting crossed legged on my bed so it wasn't hard for him to do what he intended to do. I felt an almost tingling sensation and then something else, a driving pressure. My insides felt like they were melting. I threw back my head and tried not to break hold of this erotic connection. His fingers kept moving. My system was crashing like a wave. Heat was building, and I let it consume me. Not understanding what was happening, I concentrated harder on what I was feeling. Then it happened. I exploded. Shudders passed over me and I wanted to scream. Oh my God, it felt so good. This was as good as any kill I had made, more delicious than my first taste of blood, so many years ago. This was something I could crave, just as much as the blood that I survived off of.

My hips rocked of their own accord and another wave crashed over me. It was as if I needed air in my lungs. I was parched from the heat and almost begged for more. It took a few minutes for the waves to stop, my rocking to still. I felt like I had just run for days with no break. I was spent and in awe of this new experience. Was this what it would be like to have sex? No. I knew it would be better. I had seen that much. I may be a virgin but I had lived long enough to see things that would shock the average teenage girl.

I had walked in on orgies, seen rape, and had buried the bodies of the people I had grown up with. I had seen men grunt as they rutted into a woman and didn't look away as televisions showed scenes of lovemaking. But this wasn't a moment I had ever seen before.

I gathered myself back together, like a puzzle, and asked him what had just happened. He smiled and asked if that had ever happened before.

"Of course not," I sent back, "or I wouldn't be asking."

He was surprised and then taken back.

"Oh lord, you're a virgin."

"Yes, I am."

It took him a moment to understand exactly where he stood with this and then he made his decision—it didn't matter. In fact, it was sexy as hell. He had just given me my first sexual experience and it was fuel to his flame. He was not turned off by my current status and knew he would be the one to change that. He didn't want anyone to experience what he just had. Ever. And that was fine by me.

I had just had my first orgasm and wasn't even naked. If I could have blushed then, I would have. But I hadn't fed last night, so there was no blood to rush to any part of my body. I would need to feed before going to work or I would be thirsty before the end of the night.

He raised his brow when my hunger expressed itself through our connection. He wondered what I wanted so badly. I needed to withdraw my concentration before I gave myself away. I told him I would see him later at the bar and we could actually talk then. He reluctantly agreed. I quickly sent him on his way before he picked up any other details I wasn't ready for him to see.

I got up and headed for a couple of blood bags from the fridge when I saw Perseus pacing outside of my room.

Chapter Eight

"What just happened in there?" He asked with a strained look on his face.

I was stumped for all of a second. "Do you mean about thirty minutes ago?" I asked, hoping that I was wrong.

"Yes!" He said through gritted teeth.

"Oh, that." I passed by him. He followed me to the office fridge and back.

"Excuse me, but I had the feeling that I was having an orgasm and wondered if you could tell me why," he said as he turned toward me.

He was actually tapping his foot.

I was going to enjoy this. I poured some blood into my bedside glass and made him wait for my answer.

"Most guys would love to know how that feels. And, for your information, considering it was the first one I ever had, I enjoyed it."

I was really thirsty, so I gulped down half of my glass as he stared at me.

"What?"

"I'm trying not to be dramatic and I'm having a hard time."

I giggled, and then finished my glass. But he stopped me before I could leave.

"Wait a minute. I need some explanations here."

He was back to tapping his foot, so I decided to take him seriously. I headed for another bag and motioned for him to go on.

"I feel like I need a cigarette and a nap, but considering what I am, neither is necessary. You act as if this is nothing and then you come out here and guzzle down blood like you haven't fed in days. Please explain." He ran his hands through his hair.

"Remember the thing with Angelica?"

He nodded.

"Well, apparently I can reach out to anyone I choose and they can reach me once we're connected."

He was shocked, and I continued. "That could be good or bad, depending on the situation. It works between me and you but others may be able to pick up what we are."

I shook my head and said, "I'm being careful not to think of that while I'm connected. And besides, Angelica already knew about us."

"I'm glad you can keep that out, but it concerns me that you can be reached this way. Does it go for anyone or just people close to you?"

He was clearly bothered by all of this.

"I've only done this with three people and you are one of them. And with Justin it was fabulous. All he had to do was think of touching me and I felt every bit of it. I've never had that happen before. You and I are tied and can see and feel what the other is doing, but this is beyond that. That potion intensified things for me." I finished my second glass.

"Apparently it intensified your lust in more than one aspect." He gestured toward the glass I had emptied yet again.

I then realized I had drunk two glasses in five minutes. I barely had that in one normal day. And I was still thirsty. I slid the glass away and let that fact sink in.

"Apparently so. I think I have a problem."

"What? What problem would that be? The fact that you can't stop drinking or the fact that you just had a sexual encounter without even being physically touched?"

Correction, he was immensely bothered.

"Both. And this wasn't the first time I've been touched like that." It all started to come together. "Oh shit."

He was sitting next to me before the words where completely out. His teeth were almost grinding together. "Explain."

I went back over the two times that the ghost hands had touched me. He had assumed that these occurrences had been mostly mental. I hadn't told him about the handprint on my stomach; I had unintentionally blocked him out. He wasn't happy about it.

"This isn't a good thing. This means someone has the same power as you. They could reach you before you had the power to reach them. We have no idea who this person could be or why they're playing with you. And now, you're having side effects that alter who you are."

"I know what he wants…me."

It was plain and simple. The nagging feeling I had been getting was that this person was still after me. The potion had broken their contact with me, but the problem was that I was in pain anytime that I tried to find out who it was. I would have to talk to Bambara about all of this and see what she said.

"I'll call Bambara and figure this out. She already knew most of this but the new problem needs to be brought up."

"Yes, you're right. I'll get some of the blood bags from my room and you can take them to work. I can still feel your hunger. Not good. Maybe you should take a few days off and go see Bambara in person?" He suggested as I put away my glass.

"I don't need time off when you're spreading yourself so thin. I'll call her on my way to work and see what she thinks, I promise. Let's just play this by ear and see what happens."

"Fine. But please keep me informed about all the things you experience. No more blocks. I can't help you if you're keeping me out."

I nodded and kissed him on the lips as I went to grab my things. I called Bambara before I hit the porch and she was ready for me.

"Someone has some problems," she said before I even said hello.

I smiled. "Yes, and you already have an idea about that, don't you?"

"Yes, child. I can feel your power as well as the power of the one who is chasing you. He's angry at the block between you and knows you're being helped, so he is trying to overcome that block and will do so by any means."

"You know who is responsible, don't you?"

"I believe that I do, but all will be revealed in time. I cannot tempt Fate by revealing too much of your future. It could make the situation infinitely worse. Besides, I need to do a little research on who is behind this power. Now is the time to plan, not to panic."

I walked back inside and stood by Perseus. This wasn't the type of conversation to have outside.

"Child, this man has wanted you for some time and will possess you at any cost. He'll try to finish what he started, so you'll have to possess the strength to fight him on the physical and mental planes. At this very moment, he's setting out to get back to you and I fear the worst. I can't see what will happen but I can feel the black magic he is conjuring."

Perseus spoke up. "What do we do?"

"You will need to double up on your potion and try to keep this predator away. I'm not sure if it'll be enough, but it's all I can do from here. You'll also be experiencing more side effects as we go along. I now I know that your senses have doubled, correct?"

"Yes. I woke up this morning to a driving thirst. I had more than my normal amount in just the little time since I got up."

"And you're still thirsty."

"Yes."

This worried me.

"I had hoped this wouldn't happen so soon, but it has. You'll have to feed every day to keep it at bay because the wine will only help so far and it has to be from an undiluted source. I know that is not your way but it'll keep you from becoming worse. You need to shield all people from your thoughts as to not affect them while you overcome this. Perseus will have to keep his eye out for you while these effects take place. Stay open to him so he can help you if you have any more problems."

Perseus looked grim.

"Bambara, what do I need to do right now?" I started back for the front door.

"Feed as much as possible. And stay away from people that you care about if it gets too bad because you'll hate yourself if you cross that line."

"Okay."

"Child, please be careful with who you reach out to and why. Anyone can be susceptible to your power, the more doses you take. Keep yourself isolated in as many ways as possible and I'll see if there are other ways to protect you. It requires a lot of work on my side with it being born of black magic, but I'll do it. Call me if you need me and I'll be there."

I murmured my thanks as she hung up.

We headed to work and passed Danya outside as she talked on her cell phone. Once inside, we went right to Perseus' office and he shut the door. He took several bags of blood from his briefcase and handed them to me. I wanted to tear into all of them immediately but I did as Bambara told me and I drank from one of the blood bags and put the rest in the safe since only Perseus and I had the combination. I went through the rest of the night worried over the list of side effects I had already experienced and wondered what would be added to it. At least I had something to look forward to. Not.

Justin showed up around eleven. It was slow tonight, so he came right over and got my full attention. I hugged him tight and knew I had made the right decision; we would be okay. He softly kissed my lips and I felt warm all over. I sat him down at my table and we held hands as we talked about everything. He told me about his insomnia and bad sleeping patterns then went on to explain how he turned it into a lucrative business as a specialist in night photography. He explained how he had been an only child whose parents had died young, which left him in foster care until he was a teenager. He had since lost his foster parents and had moved a few times since then.

I told him a little about my family too, but only the basics. I told him that they had been killed and that the killer had gotten away, that the only survivors had been Perseus and I, and that we stayed together because of what had happened. I explained a little about our lives since then and our few friends, namely Danya and Frank. I then went on to tell him about the new location we were to open soon.

I had a few customers that came in as we spoke, and each time I did he stepped aside and watched me work. He respected my talents but wasn't sure how far he could trust the customers. It was amusing, but knowing what I did about him, I didn't expect anything less. Just as my third customer left, Perseus handed me a large glass of blood-laced wine for me to sip on through the remainder of the evening. Everything was going fine until two am, when I felt them walk in.

It was scary how I knew it was them, and why they were here, almost immediately. Perseus came to me as fast as he sensed the trouble, but I knew not as fast as he would have liked. Thankfully, Justin stayed to the side as he chatted with Danya by the bar.

I saw Jean Luc and Giselle in the doorway and knew it was she who had changed him. She had aged a little, just as Jean Luc had. She hadn't been a vampire as long as I had, so I wondered what had happened to make her one. I couldn't read their thoughts, and that concerned me; I got the idea that they were purposely blocking me. After a few seconds of searching, a headache came on so quickly I had to stop and focused on the two people coming toward us.

"Ello lovely," Jean Luc said as he had Giselle's hand around his elbow.

She smiled and looked Perseus over.

"What can I do for you?" Perseus was trying not to sound out of character.

"Oh, we were in the area and thirsty, so we thought we would stop by," said Jean Luc as he noticed the glass in my hand.

He inhaled and knew what it was. Giselle caught the scent as well. This would be interesting. I acted casual and forced negative thoughts from my head. I'd have to start practicing on keeping people out of my head, and now was a good time to do that.

"Giselle, I haven't seen you in ages," I said to her.

She laughed. "Yes dear, it seems like decades have gone by."

"You look good. The years have been good to you."

Her face twitched. I had hit a nerve.

She cleared her throat, and Jean Luc stepped in. "Yes, although not as good as they have been to you. But we've done the best we could with what life has given us, don't you think?"

"Life has thrown us some curves but we all deal with them in our own ways."

Jean Luc knew what I meant by this.

He smiled and patted Giselle's hand. "Nice looking drink you have there. Would you happen to have a few more of those?"

"Unfortunately not. That is a special tonic that I put together for Andromeda." Perseus put a supportive hand on my shoulder.

"Well, who is this handsome young man?" Giselle reached out her other hand to Justin, "My name is Giselle Dubois and you are?"

"Justin Drake. Nice to meet you."

He shook her hand and she eyed me.

"Possibly."

"Justin is a photographer I met and he's offered to do some shots of our new place."

"Oh, you mean the place you guys bought in Louisiana? That is a nice place, we ran into your agent a couple of days ago and he was excited about the sale and must have been out spending the money he made from your purchase," Jean Luc said as he caught Perseus' eyes.

That means they either drank from him or killed him.

"He was a nice man," said Perseus.

"He was but then he suddenly got sick and had to rush home," Giselle said with a smug grin.

This meant they had fed on him and gotten information in the process.

Justin interrupted. "Excuse me. I'm going outside to take a phone call."

He sent me a mental message that he would be back but it was so faint I was lucky to have caught it.

I heard a low growl from Giselle as Justin walked away. "Mmmmm, yummy mortal. I wonder how good he tastes?"

I wasn't going to rise to the bait.

"I wouldn't know. Now what can we do for you?"

"Do I sense some hostility? Have I said something offensive?" Giselle feigned concern.

"No. We have customers and they are our concern. You are just a distraction. And you're keeping us from them." Perseus sounded bored.

Giselle let go of Jean Luc and lightly rubbed against Perseus though he retained his look of boredom as she did so.

Jean Luc pulled her back against his own body. Perseus got a little more aggressive at that point as he spoke in a low tone, his patience clearly spent. "Let's get to the point. We may live forever but we don't have all night to say whatever needs to be said."

"Now you're acting like a vampire! It's about time," said Jean Luc. "I would have used this place as a feeding ground years ago. I don't see how you pass it up. You could take people to the back and no one would ever know. You could have your choice of meat every night. But you waste it on boozers. Why?"

"Maybe he gets off on playing human, Jean Luc." Giselle was good at this game. Always had been.

"You seem to be the ones playing and I'm bored with you. State your business and leave." Perseus became more edgy with each delay.

"Ok, we'll leave. Don't start foaming at the mouth there, Pers," said Jean Luc as he put his arm around Giselle.

She said, "We'll be seeing both of you very soon."

She walked to the door and then turned to look me in the eyes.

"Next time, neither of you will be bored and I'll be the one salivating." I heard her statement in my head followed by her cackling laugh as they walked out the door.

I mentally reached for her, to see where she was going and then the pain hit me. This time it was so bad I bent over in the chair. Perseus was there and shoved the glass of blood and wine into my hands. I downed the remains and felt stable enough to walk to his office with him. He locked the door and sat me on the leather couch.

"You have about three minutes before Danya comes in here. She saw half of the conversation and then saw you bent over. I felt the pain too but couldn't tell where it was coming from. What happened?" He said as I centered myself and mentally shoved at the pain. Thankfully it decreased some.

"I'm still getting severe pains when I focus on them. It's like each attempt cracks my skull open. Bambara said they were using dark magic to connect to me and it was powerful enough to do this and more."

"Considering your increased abilities, that's a large amount of magic. You feel this pain every time you think of them? Or just when you they're present?"

"Yes to both. Whatever they're up to, they don't want me to find out about it until they're ready for me to know. But, Giselle did go so far as to threaten me before she left. Did you hear her laughing?"

"No, I couldn't hear anything but you and then I felt your pain. If you're blocking things, then that was some headache. If you weren't blocking, then you need to work harder at it because I hate to see you in that type of pain. Are you feeling any better?"

"I'm better, but I'm really tired all of a sudden. Can we just go home?"

I felt like I did when dawn approached, but I knew I had a few hours left before that happened.

"Yes, let me get this place closed up. You stay in here and rest. Here comes Danya," he got up as she came in. Seconds later, she burst in to the room.

"Are you okay? What happened?" She knelt down next to me and ran her hand over my head. "Honey, for someone who's always cold, you feel clammy."

"I have a migraine and it came on pretty fast. Sorry to frighten you, I've been getting these a little too much lately."

I mustered a small laugh but she didn't believe me.

Then she said something that made me laugh. And not stop. "Maybe your blood is low."

"You know, I think you may be right," I said, through peels of hysterical laughter.

I needed to laugh. It took my mind off the pain. "There's a wine bottle in the cabinet behind Perseus' desk. Can you pour me a glass?"

I was too weak to attempt it. She nodded and brought the glass to me. Thankfully she didn't smell the blood. My hand trembled and I dropped the wine glass before I could drink from it. It fell to the floor and broke, spilling the wine across the floor.

"Damn." I sent a plea to Perseus and knew he was rushing.

But before he could come, Danya got down on her hands and knees to mop up the mess with her bar towel. Then the unexpected happened.

"Shit, ouch. I just cut my hand on the glass stem. Now I'm going to get blood on the floor. What a mess. You're the one who feels bad and I'm the one making a bigger mess."

She kept babbling but I didn't hear a word of it. I only knew her blood. It was so sweet and heady. My throat went dry and I fought the urge to lick the red from her palm. I mentally shook myself just as Perseus came into the room. He instantly knew what was wrong and grabbed Danya's hand.

He pulled Danya out of the room as I fought to keep from feeding on my best friend's blood. This wasn't me and I refused to be a monster. It took all the strength I had, which was far too little, to fight the urge and calm down. My fangs had even come out. Thankfully, I had kept my head bent and she hadn't seen my face. Once Danya was taken care of, Perseus came back in and used his vampire skills to clean up the mess and then took the towel out to the washer. I had pulled myself together by the time he came back but was even more tired than when I'd first come in.

"She's okay but she has a one inch long cut. It's not deep enough for stitches. Justin is out there and he glued it together for her with the medical glue from the first aid kit. He did a good job; must have had some experience. Are you okay? I was afraid you were going to go for her hand."

"Me too. It was pretty intense."

"Well, I'm proud of you. You proved yet again how human you really are. You'd never willingly harm someone you love." He hugged me and a knock came through the door.

Perseus said, "Come in."

Justin walked in and stood in front of me.

"Hey, you guys had me worried there. Danya told me what happened and her friend Thomãs just showed up, so he's driving her home. She said to say sorry and good night." He knelt down to look into my face.

"Can I take you home? I want to make sure you get home safely." He held my hands and they felt so strong.

"How do you feel about that, Andy?" Perseus was, as always, worried about me.

"I'm fine. I just want to go home and sleep this headache off. I promise to be extra careful and to call you if I need you."

"Are you sure? You seemed pretty rough a little while ago."

"Yeah, I'm sure. I just want sleep, nothing else."

Perseus sighed. "Yes, please take her home. I have to cover for Danya now, so that helps us all out. I'll take her things with me when I close up. Thank you for your help. I'm glad you were here." Perseus was relieved but cautious, since we barely knew Justin. But he didn't sense anything bad, so he trusted him.

I let Justin pull me up from the couch and walk me outside to his car, that was fortunately, parked close by. I gave him the address and was so tired that I laid my head on Justin's shoulder as he put his ten-year-old burgundy Mustang in gear. Unfortunately, I wasn't too tired to notice two sets of eyes follow us as we left. I heard her laugh in my head again and then they disappeared. This was another warning and I heard her loud and clear. They had seen my weak moment and my leaving with Justin, so they'd be watching me even closer now. That meant that I'd have to protect him as well and I shivered as my mind snapped to images of him bleeding in my lap again. I'd do my best not to let my vision come true.

He pulled the car up to the house and I stumbled as I got out, very unlike me. Is this what it felt like to stay up for days on end? Where was the euphoric feeling from the other day?

He threw me up into his arms. "You aren't as light as you look, my sleeping beauty."

"Remind me to beat you later for that comment."

He laughed. "Yes ma'am."

He took out the key I had given him before we had left from his pocket and opened the front door. Once inside, he carried me up the stairs. I motioned him toward the right door, my bedroom, and was eased onto my cool bed. I sat up long enough to strip down to my camisole and panties then crawled under the covers. I didn't care that he was watching me as I stripped, and I knew he was too much of a gentleman to take advantage of the situation. I could tell, though, that he appreciated what he had seen. I snuggled into my pillow and patted the bed beside me.

"Don't leave me. Just lay here for a few minutes and I promise not to take advantage of you. I'm too tired to do anything anyway."

"Okay, as long as the rules have been set. I can spare a little more time for a damsel in distress. Mind if I get comfortable?" He waved toward his clothes, which had a small amount of Danya's blood on them.

"Yea, we don't want that in the bed, do we?"

He stripped down to his boxer briefs, laid his clothes across my vanity chair, and crawled in beside me.

He shivered for a moment. "Are you always this cold?"

I nodded against his chest and he wrapped his arms around me.

"You aren't as soft as you look either. You have a firm body."

I mumbled into his chest and he laughed.

"Yes, I will remind you to beat me later. It was a compliment, I swear. Please take it that way."

I nodded and let sleep take me over. I was dead again, but this time I had warm company and it was nice. I could get used to this.

Chapter Nine

In a warehouse by the water was a dark man with no peace or warmth. But there was plenty of rage and power, as well. Giselle and Jean Luc had come back to Captain Anastase and me. They told him what they had found out and it pleased Anastase very much.

Anastase motioned toward a whore that waited on a dusty couch, in a far corner. She sauntered over to Jean Luc and Giselle before she offered her wrists to them. They didn't hesitate and went for her tender flesh. They moaned from the opium in her blood. Anastase was always good about offering treats for a job well done. I could clearly see into the minds of these two minions. Both Jean Luc and Giselle wished that this whore was one of the people they had seen tonight. Giselle wanted Justin and Jean Luc wanted the bartender that he'd watched. Giselle always went for men out of her reach and Jean Luc loved exotic women. They both plotted to catch their prey unawares, unbeknownst by their leader.

Anastase nodded toward me, so I followed him into his temporary office and shut the door.

"Daylight is upon us and I have little time for ceremony. What will it take to break through this barrier she has around Andromeda, Olivier?" Anastase asked.

"Bambara is quite powerful but she only conjures white magic. I have surpassed that. But what you want has a price, and it is high. How badly do you want this woman?"

"I want her for all eternity. I want her more than the blood I crave. I *must* have her. And I will pay whatever price in order to have her." Anastase bowed his head to me.

"Ah, I feel your lust for her. I hope it will be worth the fee."

I pulled out a hidden altar dagger and plunged it into Anastase's chest. I purposely missed his heart but wanted the hot blood to flow. Anastase's blood was rich with the opium that he had drunk from the whore earlier in the evening and it was strong, like the pirate himself. Anastase cried out with pain and fury, but I sensed he concentrated on Andromeda to get through it. I stood in front of Anastase with a ceremonial bowl to catch the blood as it flowed out of Anastase's pain ravaged body. Giselle flew in and stood in front of Anastase's body as it bent over the bowl.

"What is this?" She screamed.

She grabbed at the dagger and I threw her away with a simple gesture of my hand. She lay in a heap and cried bloody tears for her precious master, but knew not to interfere again.

I began the incantation. The room went black. Jean Luc came in and lit a tapered candle sitting on the desk. He knew what was happening and was not about to stop it. I had let the first mate know of my intentions, as I needed a second person to ensure this ceremony went through without too many interruptions. Anastase would be close to death when I was done with him. I would not linger to put him back together. That was not my job.

Wind blew in gusts around us. Lightening flashed in the sky and through the grime coated windows. I pulled the knife out of Anastase's prone body so violently that a stream of blood squirted onto my dark face. I licked the heady blood from my full lips as I opened my robes to expose my naked flesh. I drew the bloody knife across my chest in the pattern of an X, and both bloods mingled.

I put my calloused fingers into Anastase's open wound and fervently pressed as I continued my chanting. His obsidian eyes rolled into the back of his head. Lightning struck the building. Giselle screamed and Anastase moaned. At that very moment, I drove my hand further into Anastase's quaking body. The captain screamed for his immortal soul. Pulling out my hand, I threw the bloody tissue from my hand and into the awaiting bowl. I grabbed the leather pouch tied at my thick neck and dumped the contents into the bowl as well and Anastase's body dropped to the cold floor.

Jean Luc came over and set the bloody contents in the bowl on fire with the already lit candle and then stepped back. Anastase released another scream as his body convulsed and the smoke encircled his tortured body. He shook so badly that his teeth rattled. Giselle sobbed Anastase's name from her corner. Lightning struck one last time and I yelled over the sound toward Anastase.

"Who do you want?" I commanded of Anastase.

Anastase moaned, "Andromeda Ortiz."

He convulsed one last time before he passed out.

Giselle screamed, "No!" and ran toward Anastase's unresponsive body.

Blood ran in a stream of tears down her face and onto Anastase's open wound.

"Why did you do this? You don't need her, you stupid pirate. I wished she'd never woken up from the sea that I threw her to, all those years ago. You were supposed to see that I was the only one for you" Then to me, "What have you done to him? He's not healing."

"He wanted the gypsy woman and was willing to pay the price. I needed his blood to enforce the bond. He knew what he was doing and now he must take time to heal. He will need plenty of blood and can have opium for the pain. The dagger tears even immortal flesh, and it drains the power of the one it pierces. He will be himself in a few days. Watch him well."

I wiped the blood from the knife and closed my robe, and then walked out into the approaching dawn. It was like the storm had never been there. Such was my power.

As I moved onward, I could sense the emotions rolling through the infuriated Giselle. Anastase had sold a piece of his immortal soul for a woman who didn't even want him. All she knew was that someone would pay for this betrayal. She would kill Andromeda and take her place back at Anastase's side, for all eternity. No one would stand in her way. But her feelings were nothing to me. I had my own prey. Vengeance would rule, soon.

As, I disappeared into the shadows, I saw Giselle clearly in my mind. She wiped the bloody tears away and bit into her wrist. As the blood seeped out, she placed it over the hole in her master's chest. It seemed to help, but only slightly. As I had known would happen. She carried him to her black SUV and was to drive him back to her rented loft on Tybee Island. Her plan was to take him to her bedroom and try to get him to bite her. But I knew that he would still be unconscious, so she would have to start an IV bag of blood. This was the only way to replenish a vampire's sleeping body once this much damage had been inflicted. With what I knew of her, she would cling to the man who had betrayed her, as she succumbed to the daytime sleep of the eternal dead.

Darkness shrouded me and I embraced my power as I waited to take Bambara's life.

* * * *

Justin woke up just after I did. We smiled at the fact that we had unintentionally slept together all night. I was thirsty with my need to feed. Perseus was going to have to supply more blood bags until I got through this; I was almost thirsty enough to be distracted from the sexual tension coming from Justin.

Justin pressed me to his warm body. He was almost as hard as I was. This was interesting. I wondered if I could take advantage of this situation when I was so thirsty. There was only one way to know.

I reached my face up to his and pushed my lips against his. He kissed me right back and it was wonderful and went on and on. I didn't want him to stop. I got more passionate and started kissing him more fervently as I crawled on top of him. I pressed his shoulders down and traced my tongue over his mouth. Then I darted my tongue between those soft lips and laved my tongue all over their interior.

It wasn't enough. I slid my legs around his waist and felt my hair sweep over his chest. His moan drove me to push my crotch on top of his erection, rocking gently. He gasped. I laughed as I nipped his lip. I let my weight fall on top of him as I rolled my hips, increasing the tempo. I licked those lips and tasted his blood. Oh, it was so delicious. I started to suck on that lip until I finally noticed he was pushing back at me.

Oh my God, I was feeding on his torn lip. What had I done? I jumped off him a little too quickly for a mortal. He sat up and licked the drop of blood from his lip. It made me cringe.

"I am so sorry, Justin. I don't know what got into me," I lied. I knew what was wrong and I had crossed a line that he didn't even know existed.

"It's okay, you just surprised me. I didn't expect you to be so aggressive and strong." He tried to laugh it off.

I saw my palm prints on his shoulder from where I had pushed him down. Not good. I gnawed on my own lips and realized my fangs were still half way out, so I quickly covered my mouth and mumbled something about morning breath then shut myself into the bathroom. I called to Perseus and told him I had sucked on Justin's bitten lip with my partially exposed fangs. I kept my mouth shut as I came back out of the bathroom. A knock came to my bedroom door.

"Morning. Are you guys decent?"

He came in and had a mug in each of his hands. I smelled the blood he had poured into my favorite cup; it was dark with it. He handed me my cup and the other to Justin with a kind smile.

"Sorry to interrupt but I wanted to check on Andromeda after last night. I thought I'd bring in some coffee and see how she was doing. Andy, when you feel better, I need some help today."

I drank down the coffee, which would suffice for now.

"Yes, thank you. Do you need me to help with the new place?"

"I'm afraid so. I have several employees to check out and then call the best ones to see when they can start. Would you mind terribly if I kept you from Mythology for tonight?"

He looked sincere but I knew he wanted me to stay away from people until I got myself under control. I didn't want to take the day off, but I couldn't trust myself. If I could bite Justin, then I could do it to anyone. I gave the cup back to Perseus.

"Yes, I feel better and I'll help you tonight. I need to get dressed, either way." I laughed and used this as an excuse to get Justin out.

I put my arm around Justin as he got up from the bed and grabbed his clothes. He didn't seem to care that he only wore his boxer briefs. He dressed quickly and I gave him a spare toothbrush. Perseus grabbed the blood bag from his pants pocket and quickly handed it to me. I drained it before Justin finished brushing his teeth. I slipped the empty plastic under the blanket and hugged him as he came out.

"Justin, thank you for staying with me last night. I'll call you later and we'll make plans to hang out soon, okay?" He nodded and hugged me back.

He also went in for a kiss but I kept it chaste, as I knew I had blood on my breath. I walked him to the door, and hugged him again before he reluctantly left.

"I'm glad we got rid of him without any problems. That could've gotten ugly. Are you that bad you bit him?"

I nodded.

"Well, you need to feed. And staying here would make things safer for everyone. I don't want you heading out to feed all by yourself, so I'll get more blood for you. You don't have too much self control, which makes me worry about what else might happen."

I had to agree with him and went back to change. I wore leggings and a flowing tunic blouse with a low cowl neckline. I met Perseus at the front door so we could feed before he headed to the bar. I wasn't too happy about having to be chaperoned but I understood why.

I held his hand on the porch and concentrated. I saw in my mind a man who sold drugs under the bridge by the interstate. I went there but didn't know that I had left Perseus behind until I was standing alone. The drug dealer lit a cigarette and went back to his hidden spot in the shadows.

I wondered if I had gone to a separate place or if I had somehow stopped Perseus from coming with me. I followed the path that went under the bridge and saw the young man stand up against the cold concrete wall. He nodded at me, not knowing if I could see him in the darkness, but I saw his every feature.

He had deep set, slanted eyes. He was shorter than me and had asymmetrically cut black hair. I was surprised that he did well with his business since he was so young looking, but he must have a clientele to be sitting out here waiting.

I quietly stepped closer and he asked what I needed. Oh, what I need. I could feel the throb of his blood. It made my mouth salivate. My teeth extended. His heart sped up as his eyes adjusted to seeing my toothy grin.

"You aren't one of my regulars," he said as he stomped on his cigarette butt.

"No, I'm not."

"Well, then what can I do for you? Do you need X, meth, something spicier?"

I smiled. "Mmmmm, spicier."

I could taste him as he stood just inches from being my prey.

He stood away from the wall and named off his inventory. He was well stocked. I just shook my head.

"Lady, I have all this stuff and there is nothing there that you're interested in?" He asked in surprise.

"There is something I'm interested in. But it wasn't in your inventory, no matter how impressive your list is."

I felt his heart beat faster and I had to swallow at the feeling it invoked. I stepped closer to him and breathed in his scent. He smelled of soy sauce, strong tea and unfiltered cigarettes. I heard him gulp as I took another step closer. Apparently he was used to quick and impersonal transactions; I made him nervous.

"Sorry if I don't have what you need. Ivan on Union Street has a few other items of interest. You can tell him that I sent you."

He thought he could dismiss me so easily.

"You misunderstood me. You have what I need."

My voice got huskier with my need.

"But you didn't want anything I mentioned, so what do you want?"

He stepped backwards; I took one big step toward him. We were nose to nose by the time his last word got out. He yelped.

"Look lady, I don't know what you need but I ain't got it. Just step off and get the fuck out of here. "

He pulled out an old fashioned razor from his pocket and I allowed him the second it took for him to open it. The next thing he knew, his hand was bleeding where I had yanked it from his grasp. He screamed. I grabbed his mouth in one hand and dropped the blade. I smelled his blood as it trickled from his palm to the ground. What a waste.

I pushed him between my body and the stone wall, like being between a rock and a hard place. I giggled with my inside joke and pulled his hand toward my mouth. He shoved at me with his uninjured hand, but to no avail. I drug my wet tongue across the sticky blood and moaned. I was going way too far with this kid but I didn't care. My hunger kept me moving forward.

I had him crushed against me with nowhere to go and no one to help him. It was so easy. He was trying everything he could to move me but it wasn't going to happen. He started to hyperventilate, which was fine with me. I started to suck up the blood. He passed out, his body limp against mine. I leaned him against the slanted wall as I sucked the blood from his open palm. It was so good. I sank my teeth into that smooth skin. I couldn't get enough. My brain had to fight against the tempting thought of drinking this young man dry. I stopped just before the last drop and laid him across the floor just as Perseus came to stand behind me.

"Please tell me you didn't kill him."

"No, he'll sleep this off and think it was a nightmare." I replied as I clotted the blood with my tongue.

I placed the razor next to him on the ground, so it looked as if he had dropped it as he had passed out. Perseus grabbed my arm and pulled me up toward him.

"How did you get here without me and what did you do to him?"

"I saw him in my mind, like I usually do, and then I was here. I did like I usually do; I drank from him. He isn't dead. I didn't do anything ugly to him," I said defensively.

"Why is his hand bleeding and where did the razor come from?"

"He pulled the razor on me and I took it from him. That's where I fed from." I was exasperated by him. "Look, you're my twin and can usually see what's going on with me. Why are you questioning me?"

"Sis, I was going somewhere else. I couldn't follow you for several minutes. You had blocked me out, somehow. I couldn't read your thoughts, feel your emotions or see where you went. I had to concentrate on just you and then I was dragged here."

"*Oh.*"

Now I understood why he was worried. He was trying to chaperone me and I had somehow stopped him from doing that. These kinds of side effects were not as cool as the ones I had with Angelica and Justin.

A little angry, I said, "There has to be yin with yang. I know that doesn't make sense to you but I can't change what happened and I can't stop everything that this mess is throwing at me. Just back off and we'll get through this."

I was ready to leave.

"So, you have severe hunger and blocking as your bad side affects and nothing else?"

"Nothing else. That's more than enough to deal with right now."

"What parts do you consider yang?"

I squeezed his hand and thought of kissing Angelica and my orgasm with Justin. This time he got the images and nodded.

"I can see how those would be the better part. You can portray all of these emotions to me now, but you can also block me out completely. That isn't good."

I rubbed at the frown line in his forehead, to stop it from getting deeper and smiled at him.

"You should talk, Mr. Suffer in Silence. At least this was unintentional."

I flew us out of there without his help. We stopped in the park by my favorite cemetery. I thought it would be a good place to talk for a moment. I held his hand as we walked. People walking by might find this image of us walking here scandalous, but I felt at peace, so I began my speech.

"I know we have to get to the bottom of this. I'm sorry that I have enough power to block you. I have no idea what other things I can do. I reached a limit with that kid back there and before with Justin in my bedroom. I have no idea if it'll get worse or what will happen next. I'll try to maintain my connection to you so you can see if I get into any more trouble but it's hard to harness this."

He nodded. We walked out of the cemetery and toward the house. I could sense that he was upset for the way he had treated me. That helped clear my conscious a little bit.

"I need you to make some calls for me while I go to work. Do you think you will be okay tonight? Do I need to stay with you?"

"I've fed and will stay in the house just to make sure I don't have any more problems. If I feel anything strange, I'll call you. I've got this. Please don't feel that you have to baby sit me."

That was all he could ask for, under the circumstances, so he walked me to the porch and left for the bar. I stepped in and heard him in my head as I locked up.

"Please make the calls that I have on the dinning room table and make any notes you feel necessary. Thank you."

I agreed and went into the dining room to start my work. I hated to be at home when I could be at work, but I was more concerned about my actions the last few hours. Was it going to get worse? I called Bambara but she didn't answer her phone. I couldn't reach her mentally so I left her alone. She must be in the middle of something important for me not to be able to reach her.

I started calling all the applicants that Perseus had marked and a majority of them were available immediately. Most of the references checked out and it seemed to be going well. My cravings kicked up a notch as I jotted down notes, so I fixed myself a glass of tainted wine but it didn't fulfill my need. I went to Perseus' room to get a blood bag from his cabinet. I topped off my glass and sipped at it. It curbed my need, but only just. I went downstairs and relaxed on the couch as I finished my notes.

I thought of Frank and his help with our employment and immediately saw him in his office. He was shocked as he felt me there, I laughed since this was a fun part of my new power. I whispered hello and he returned the greeting. He spoke in a whisper inside his office, as if I stood next to him.

"Ms. Ortiz, am I to believe this is part of your new liquid diet?"

"Yes. I've had several changes, but this is a perk."

I was showing off and I knew it.

"I see. What can I do for you?"

"I was going over the employee list and most of these are very promising. I wanted to thank you for your effort in our new location."

"You are most welcome, anything for one of my colleagues. Is there anything else you needed?"

"No, but thank you for asking."

"I hope they are to your liking and do you a great service."

I thought of the service I had gotten from Angelica and had to stop myself so he wouldn't see that image.

"Well, I'll let you get back to work. I'll call you if anything else is needed and thank you again."

"Anytime, Ms. Ortiz."

I let him go and let my mind wander as I slid down into the comfortable cushions. I thought of Justin and saw him taking pictures of the full moon. I didn't want to interrupt his concentration so I backed away from him before he noticed me. I thought about Angelica and saw her asleep in her bedroom. There were boxes around the bed, so I knew she was ready to move to the apartment she had found near the club. She was going to like it there.

She smiled in her sleep and murmured my name, so I knew she felt me there. I smiled and whispered good night. She rolled over and went back to sleep. I felt her peace and it was a nice thing to feel after the last few hours. I watched her in her peacefulness for a few minutes before starting to drift off myself.

Chapter Ten

It was a pull, like when dawn called to me. I was relaxed enough to enjoy it. I must be getting tired easier, now that I had all these strange side effects. I felt like I was being carried somewhere by a gentle wind. I sighed and gave myself up to its gentle touch.

I heard a male voice whisper my name. I didn't know who it was but it seemed very familiar to me. The wind turned into fingers, gliding over my body. It reminded me of when Justin had touched me through my gift. I thought of him doing this to me and realized that maybe I hadn't broken the connection between us as I had thought that I had.

I stretched like a cat as fingers traced my body. I murmured his name and heard his lazy laugh as the fingers grew more insistent. They played with the neckline of my tunic then tugged at the layers that held it in place. The silky fabric slid down. I arched to let it fall around my ribcage. I heard a hiss and felt the leather strap of Bambara's necklace fall to the floor. I lay back against the cushions that felt more like clouds in my dream state and relished the feeling of his touch.

I felt feather light touches at my neck and turned my head to accommodate. Tiny kisses were placed at my neck. My dusky nipples tightened. I whimpered a little as the pressure of the kisses grew. It felt so real. He nipped his way down over the column of my throat and down to my collarbone. I felt a small nip there and gasped.

I gripped the cushion under me as he nipped his way down toward my naked breasts. I arched upward, off of the couch as he reached my waiting nipple. It was as if I was thrusting it into his warm mouth. I moaned as I felt his tongue encircle its hardness.

Warmth flowed through my core as he became more aggressive. I felt a hand on my other breast as it flicked at that lonely nipple. I ached for more. I felt the other hand as it pushed me into the deep cushions. I needed more. My animal side was hungry. I had denied it for too long.

I threw my head back as I felt a wet tongue flick over both aching breasts, in turn. I wanted to shove them back into his mouth; I didn't care how wanton I was. I felt like I was melting as he took the second one into his mouth for the same torture he had given the first one. I whispered the word "*More*" and heard him laugh.

He wanted me to feel this way and I had no problem expressing it. He ran his mouth back to the first hard nipple. I gasped again when he sucked on its hardness. I heard him whisper my name before he bit the tip of my nipple. It was exquisite torture. I arched against his hand and pressed my nipple against his teeth, rubbed it across that jagged surface.

I felt an irregular bump to those teeth. I tried to scream but he instantly muffled my cry. I felt those fangs sink lower through my marble flesh. This wasn't Justin at all. I tried to thrash but was being held tight against my sinful prison.

I was too close to climaxing and when he drew on my breast, I exploded. I went in one big shudder as I felt my blood being drawn from that traitorous nipple, with ghost fangs deep in my flesh. I didn't know I was capable of this, let alone from a ghostly vampire stalker. I moaned as it crashed through me. The mouth still pulled. I could feel it straight from my heart, as he drew ravenously from me. I began to black out and fought it as so much blood was robbed from me.

The other hand pinched my other nipple in a crushing pressure. I climaxed harder but I fought it this time. This was wrong on so many levels. The mouth drew so deeply that I could feel my life's blood sprinting out of me as the hand squeezed tight enough to crush it. I cried out against the hand over my mouth and thought of Perseus. I couldn't see his face as I grew weak, but I knew he felt me in distress and was coming to help me.

I could feel the anger of my attacker as he realized what I had done. He stopped sucking and the waves started to abate. He laughed, as he knew how my body had betrayed me and whispered, "I will be back, my love. You cannot stop me." And then I passed out.

It seemed like forever but it must have been only minutes before I saw Perseus sitting on the couch by my legs. I saw myself through his eyes as I lay there, limp and a trickle of blood running down my naked nipples. There were puncture wounds on one and the other one was seriously bruised. He gathered his senses and wiped away the blood with his handkerchief before he tried to pull my blouse up higher. This task was difficult since the blouse lay crumpled under my heavy body.

He grabbed the lap blanket off the armrest behind himself and covered me up. I looked dreadful. I couldn't open my eyes and I saw through his eyes that I was pale, almost a blue tone. He grabbed my hand and squeezed as he whispered my name. He felt my presence but knew I had been drained of too much blood to respond fully. I tried to squeeze his hand. He ran to his room for two bags of blood. He ripped one open before he even sat down on the couch.

He tilted my head back and nudged my lips open. It was hard to even swallow, but I did it with his encouragement. I was too tired to rouse myself from this lethargic state. The only thing that kept me conscious was the awareness that I had been violated. I felt the blood flow through me. I was more coherent by the time he got the second bag to my lips. I had the strength to open my eyes as I finished. I saw the concern in Perseus' eyes as I fought to keep mine open. He leaned me back against the pillows and covered me back up as he reached for his phone.

I heard him talk to Bambara about how he'd found me. I could feel her reaching out to me mentally. The conversation was brief and he hung up after he promised to call her back. Apparently, they had no idea what had happened but somehow my stalker had broken through the barrier and had fed from me. This would bind us further and meant I'd have to take more potion to strengthen the wall that had been put between us.

They had debated a source to use to try and stop him and decided it had to be a mortal with blood untainted by any drugs. Angelica was too far away to help me and some people lied about their habits. Bambara suggested Danya or Justin. Perseus quickly objected since neither knew what we are. She suggested that they be compelled into forgetting it and knew we wouldn't harm them. He still didn't like the idea but knew I had to drink the potion soon. My mind flickered back to almost biting Justin in my bedroom. I was concerned that I would not be able to stop, but I also knew I would do what was needed in order to keep from getting worse or from harming anyone unduly. Then I thought of it.

"Transfusion," I whispered.

Perseus thought over the idea and called Bambara back. They decided it was worth a try since blood was screened before being bagged, and I wouldn't be able to harm my victim this way. But he'd have to get several more bags of blood due to my increased hunger. He didn't want to leave me alone so he got my cell phone and called Justin. I was apprehensive about Justin being here and I hoped that I'd be too weak to harm him.

On the phone, Perseus told Justin that I had contracted a type of blood virus that could make me suddenly weak and required special fluids. He explained to Justin that it wasn't contagious and that I got sick from time to time because of it. Perseus needed someone to watch over me while he went to get my, so-called, medicine and an IV prepared. Justin was leery about what could be ailing me but agreed to come right over.

I was in a haze from my debilitated state. I could hear what was going on but didn't have the strength to participate. I hated being this weak and I hadn't felt this bad since I'd been changed. I felt Perseus lift me in his arms and carry me upstairs to my room. He gently laid me on my covers and removed my remaining clothing. I couldn't help him a bit as he dressed me in a chocolate brown silk gown and slid me under the covers.

He kept looking at my face as he waited and I saw myself through his eyes again. I still had a blue tint to my skin, but not as bad anymore. I looked more like I had been sick for a few days. The gown hid the mark plus any blood that would be spilled on it while I had my IV. Thankfully the bed linens were dark hunter green; white fabric would be a bad idea right now.

My brother knew that we didn't have enough blood in the house to meet my needs, so he was going to have to go get some from the source he had at the blood bank. One of these bags would have to have the potion injected into it for the transfusion to be effective. He called his source and had several bags being hidden for our use.

Perseus pulled up my overstuffed Victorian chair next to the bed and rubbed my hand until he heard Justin pull up. He rushed down to meet Justin and pulled him in for a quick talk before they headed back upstairs. I strained to hear them as Perseus warned Justin about how bad I looked. Justin was confused at how I got sick so quickly. He went over the illness he had made up for me and it was very persuasive. Perseus explained that the sooner the fluid was administered, the faster I'd get better. At that explanation, Justin rushed up the stairs so Perseus could be on his way.

I heard his quick intake of breath when he saw me lying there. He quietly walked to my side, so as not to wake me. Once he was seated, I slowly slid my hand across the covers toward him. He grabbed it up and held my cold hand between his two warm ones.

"Honey, I just saw you. I can't believe you went down hill this quickly."

"Didn't you notice how funny I acted before? It was coming on then, and last night I was too tired to move. Things like this happen and I have to fix it quickly. Perseus knows what to do."

It all came out as a whisper but Justin had caught my words. He squeezed my hand and didn't want me to talk too much.

I dozed in and out for a while and felt my strength coming back in inches. By the time I felt Perseus come home, I was trying to push myself up against the antique headboard. Justin caught my movements and helped me. I was a little heavy in my weakened state so Justin slid behind me in order to hold me upright. When Perseus came into the room he was surprised to see us in bed together. I mentally told him I felt better and wanted to sit up.

"Andromeda, you shouldn't be doing too much right now," he said to me and then to Justin, "I'm not sure if you want to be in here for this but I'm about to insert an IV into her arm."

He didn't hear any complaints and got right to work.

Justin put his arms around my waist as the IV needle went in. Of course, the needle was special; an ordinary one would have bent or broken from the strength of my skin. The bag of tainted blood had been covered as to not give away the dark red color that came from the potion that was mixed with it, proof that Perseus had thought this out completely. I felt a rush go through my body as the potion started to seep in with the IV open all of the way. I sighed and settled into Justin as I dozed off. I started to drift in and out of sleep but could hear them talk about me every once in awhile.

I heard Perseus ask Justin about his life and Justin wanted to know about my childhood. I heard Perseus explain my childhood, our childhood, and how things had changed those many years ago. I was a simpler version of myself back then.

Of course, my thoughts flowed to the day I met the vampire pirate from my past. I saw his blond hair, blowing in the wind as he stood on his ship. His sadistic smile that had been full of charm; he was a very impressive figure. He was quite handsome, for a devil. If it had been any other circumstance then I would've been drawn to him, but knowing what he was had changed that. I drifted deeper as I wondered what had happened to him. Had he sailed the seas until his demise or was he still out there?

* * * *

I unwittingly reached further into my memories of him, and I felt an ache in my chest. Then I saw him. It was a more modern time. He was dressed in jeans and a black polo shirt. It was night and he was on a ship, but not the one I had been on. This one was steel and larger, like a freight ship. He turned and it seemed as if he was looking directly at me. That was strange. I must be dreaming.

He shook his head at me.

"What? Do you know what I'm thinking?"

He nodded.

This was freaking me out. He smiled that heart-stopping smile of his. There was no doubt that he was indeed hearing my thoughts. He stepped closer to me and I was pulled onto the ship with him. He was just inches away from me and I couldn't move. I was still wearing the brown silk gown and the wind whipped it around my body.

He reached out to me. I couldn't move my feet but I could use my hands, until he grabbed both of my wrists. He held them next to my body and leaned down toward me. In that instant he changed into the pirate who had made me a vampire. He was even wearing the same tunic and pants from back then, with scabbard and scarf at his hip. What had happened?

"It's time for you to know your fate, my beauty," he said softly through his exposed fangs.

"What's happening, Anastase?"

"You will call me Damien. Now that you have finally come to me you'll know what I have planned for us."

"I don't understand."

He nodded. "I'm sorry, I drank too deeply and you're not prepared for this. But never the less, you are here."

Oh my God. I had thought that it was a stranger, or even a sick joke by Jean Luc. I hadn't put the clues together enough to even contemplate it being Anastase.

"You. You were the one behind all of this? You were the one who's been stalking me and drank from me?"

That explains the power and the blood he drew. I had let this man touch me, mentally and physically. Even worse, I had wanted him to do those things to me. I was disgusted with myself.

"Yes, my dear. I've looked for you for many years and now I have you. You're just as beautiful as you were back then. I see you still have that same fire in your soul."

"Am I supposed to be flattered?"

He chuckled. "No, my dear. I'd expect you to be indifferent. You never did realize the power you had over men, mortal or not, even Jean Luc wants you."

"I thought Jean Luc was the one doing all this. I never would've thought that you'd have the nerve to face me again."

He pulled me up against his hard body.

"Lady, I have more than nerve. I've wanted you for hundreds of years and I have no intention of letting you slip away again."

I tried to be calm about this because I needed to know what his plans were.

"You sent Jean Luc and Giselle to find me?"

"In a way, yes, I did. After years of searching, I found out where you lived. When we were brought here on business, it fit two purposes." He leaned closer to me, barely an inch away from my face. "My God, you are truly breathtaking."

I couldn't fight him, even if I wanted to. Just as his lips came down, I knew he had power over my body. He crushed me to him and took possession of my lips in a hungry kiss. I could do nothing but let him ravage my mouth. I wanted to feel revulsion or anger but none of it would come to me. Why couldn't I fight him? Why did my body want to join in? This was sheer madness.

His fangs pushed against my lips and they opened of their own accord. I had lost control of everything but my mind. I felt his fangs rub against my lips as his hunger grew. Just when I thought he would bite my lips, he ran his tongue over them instead. He seemed to be savoring this and had no intention of drawing blood, yet. My arms automatically wrapped around his waist. He smiled against my lips.

I wanted him to kiss me, badly, but why? My body took over and I opened my mouth fully to him. He devoured my mouth as if he was ravenous. I'd never kissed a vampire before. Perseus had told me that being with a vampire was much more intense than regular experiences, that it could make you do things you'd never dreamed. He had loved his trysts with other vampires and had suggested I have one as my first. But this was not the man I wanted.

I tried to fight as I thought of Justin. I whispered his name and felt Anastase's fury at the mere mention of another man. He crushed me as tight as he possibly could. A mortal would have died under that amount of pressure. One arm kept me at his side as the other snaked up to caress my face. His tongue danced with mine. I felt his hand in my hair and it caressed my scalp as he increased the pressure. My skin was on fire. It wasn't like it had been with Justin. This was fierce and anger, where Justin was passion and need. Although I didn't know how or why, I wanted them both, but for different reasons. As his cruel mouth ran kisses down the column of my exposed neck, I had the chance to ask him.

"What madness have you driven me to, Anastase?"

His free hand was at my shoulder and he no longer needed to hold me prisoner against his body.

"Damien," he corrected me again.

I shook my head. I wouldn't give him more power over me and using his name would do just that. It was a small victory but I would take it.

"My dear, I have used old magic to bind us and we're together in almost every way. I can feel your needs, hear your thoughts and see what you do. You belong to me." He whispered the last few words against my collarbone.

I felt the strap of my gown slip down to my elbow. I gasped when he held my breast in his hand. He intended to do more. I was a slave to him. Then, as I looked down, I saw the puncture wounds and reality hit me. This was how he had bound me, by drinking my blood. I couldn't let him do it again and make his connection stronger. I had to get out of this. His tongue ran over my once again traitorous body and his fangs glided over my nipple.

A silent scream ripped through me as the sound was held in the prison walls of my body. I thought of Perseus, Bambara, Danya, and Justin. Just as his teeth started to re-enter my wound I screamed for Perseus. I felt a pull from my center. I heard a cry of rage as I was pulled from the scene of my madness and back into my own bed. I felt arms around me. I screamed.

"Andy, please wake up."

I was being shaken. I forced my eyes open and gasped as I saw my brother lean over me. I also realized that I was still in my own bed and lying against Justin's strong chest.

"Andy, are you ok?" Perseus asked.

I could see myself in his eyes and I looked frantic. He had leaned over the bed as Justin held me still against his body. Then I felt it, the blood at my breast. I sat up and yanked the fabric down, while Justin fought to calm me. There was the truth, the spots of fresh blood against my nipple. I had stopped him from drinking this time, just barely. I heard Justin asking what I was doing and if I was okay. He thought I had been having a nightmare. I truly had been.

I said to Perseus, "It was him. Anastase."

I had the strength to send him the images, no matter how much I hated what I had done. He stared into my eyes as he absorbed what had happened.

Justin was clueless about our tragic past, but I was giving way too much about my real life already. I quickly covered up and silently leaned back into Justin's arms.

"I'm okay, it was a nightmare. Thank you for getting me out of it." I meant it in more than one way.

Perseus wasn't able to say anything further with Justin there. He let me know that he had felt my panic and had used his mind to link with Bambara's before pulling me out. Perseus excused himself and I knew he was headed to call Bambara. She would need to know what had happened. I noticed that the IV had been taken out. I felt more like myself but I still needed to rest. I decided I would sleep the morning away and see how things were tomorrow night.

Justin rubbed my hair as I relaxed against him. It was a reassuring feeling that distracted me from my layers of self-loathing and anger for letting Anastase touch me. I had betrayed both Justin and myself. I'd have to come to terms with these warring emotions. I also knew this would bring questions from Justin. At this very moment I sensed he wondered what had happened and who Anastase was. He wanted to know what I had looked at when the blanket had been pulled away. He hadn't seen or heard all of what had happened and would ask his questions when I was stronger, or when Perseus would honestly answer them.

Justin stayed with me that following day and I slept restlessly. I was afraid to dream but too tired to fight it. I awoke early the next night and noticed two things, the yearning I had for the man curled up against me, and my harrowing lust for blood. I wasn't sure which was greater or which I'd quench first. Of course, there was the simple fact that this man could provide me with both, but that was difficult for my mind to comprehend. I could seduce him, drink his blood and then compel him into only remembering the sex part. Would I feel guilty afterward? Or would that entice my dark side to only do it again at a later date.

This would be easier if he knew what I was and could decide for himself if he wanted our relationship to function this way. I needed to tell him, no matter how mad it made Perseus. This affected my life more than my brother's, and it was wrong to keep deceiving this wonderful man. I made a promise to myself right then that I'd tell Justin within the next few days and let the cards fall where they would.

* * * *

My face was lying on his chest. I slid my face slowly from his skin. He was sleeping so soundly that I almost hated to touch him. Almost. The need in me was too great to deny. The potion had indeed worked and I was feeling everything. Something had cracked in my control and I had to give into my needs. I ran my lips just barely over the surface of the skin I had just lain on. It was a feather light touch and I wasn't sure if he'd feel it. I kissed up and down his chest until his eyes twitched. I knew I was getting somewhere when there was a slight rise in the covers below his waist.

Placing small kisses along that same line brought a soft moan from him. I put more pressure behind the kisses and moved them in random areas around his chest and then finally settled on the nipple closest to me. He gasped when I placed a wet kiss there. I felt completely brazen. I took that dusky pink nipple into my mouth, lightly suckled it. He balled his fist around the covers. I was on the right track.

I sucked harder, until I heard the air rushing into his lungs. I moved over his body and ended up lying on top of him with my hands positioned on each side of his face. I drug my hair up across that wet nipple and took my time as I went. By the time I was even with his face, his eyes had popped open. The dark haze I saw there was more than just sleep; it was the same hunger that I felt burning at my soul. I repeated my previous action across his face, until I came to his parted lips. I kissed him lightly and realized that he wasn't taking any action what so ever. He was letting me make all the moves. This was both interesting and empowering.

Chapter Eleven

My wild side kicked in and I dove in for a passionate kiss. His toes actually curled. He breathed heavily and I knew I had to remember that he needed air more than I did. I ran my tongue over his full lips until he groaned and then kissed him again. By this time he was reaching for my hips. I let him hold me to his growing hardness. I rubbed myself against it and heard him moan again. I leaned over and took his other nipple into my mouth. I sucked it harder than the first one; his grip tightened on my hips.

Strategically I shrugged my shoulders so the silk of my gown would slip lower, down to my elbows, exposing my own hard nipples to his gaze. He didn't move so I leaned over and put one aching nipple right against his lips. Rubbing it back and forth felt spectacular but not as good as I needed it to be. Putting my weight into it, I slid my nipple down his mouth until his lips separated to encircle it. His teeth remained closed. I rubbed that bud against his even teeth as heat began to spread through me. Very slowly he opened his mouth and took me into his mouth. I arched into him. I may be in a lifestyle where sucking is required, but this was heaven. I didn't know my marble skin could ache like this.

It was torture when he stopped but he wrapped one hand around that breast to insert the other nipple into his mouth for the same delicious treatment. After several minutes of this I was ready to explode and didn't realize that he had only just begun. He surprised me by flipping us over onto my back. He kissed me deeply before running his hard tongue down the center of my chin, down over my neck, between my breasts and into my navel.

My core had heated up and it wanted to consume me. He laved that tongue over the skin of my stomach before trailing lower still. I was beside myself when he made a wet path to my womanhood and drove his tongue inside. I tore at the sheets and had to remember to restrain my strength. I could have broken both him and the bed at that point. I had no idea what he was doing but I was on the brink of madness. Heat expanded down my legs. I quivered.

How could a vampire quiver? Then I exploded. This orgasm was stronger than my previous one. I arched off of the bed and fisted the covers. He pulled away from me for a moment and I heard a rustle but didn't open my eyes to see what was going on. The waves of pleasure were so strong that I wanted to die from them.

I felt him climb up the bed and lay his naked body on top of mine. He captured an aching nipple in his mouth and bit down just as he entered my body. I came off the bed, taking him with me. I bit my lip to hold in my scream. He began to thrust into me with enough pressure to make my wet body tighten up, but he didn't release my nipple. It was exquisite pain and pleasure.

After a moment he drove harder and took the other nipple into his mouth as I rocked with him. It wasn't enough. I drove myself against him until I climaxed again. This time I moaned so loud that it echoed off of the walls. My mind exploded just as his mouth closed over my own in a savage kiss. I held on to his slick body, following his lead. He pushed one last time, moaned into my open mouth then arched off of me as he came. We both lay back against each other as the waves died back down and the earth went back on its normal axis.

Would it be like this every time? Was this what it felt like to lose your virginity? I had heard that it was painful and awkward but this was the complete opposite. I had also heard about blood and your body ripping, but was that true for a vampire? I guess I would find out, once I managed to move. I inwardly laughed at how wonderful I felt. This was far better than the high I had gotten off of drinking from Angelica. I had so many questions.

It was amusing when I saw Justin shift his position. He thought he was too heavy to lie on top of me. Then he squirmed for a moment and got off of the bed. Oh, how sweet. He had put on a condom and was getting rid of it before he came back to bed. I knew without a doubt that I loved this man.

Before he came back to the bedroom I saw one small bead of blood drying on the sheet. I covered it up quickly as he came back into my bedroom. He was feeling no shame and was happy with being my first lover. I heard his thoughts as he scrambled for the right words for this moment. I scooted over in the bed and curled up to him. I still had a few minutes before I had to get ready for work and I wanted to relish this stolen moment.

"Are you okay?" He twirled my hair around his finger.

"Yes, I'm wonderful," I purred.

"I was trying to distract you from the pain and had hoped I wasn't being too aggressive."

"I'm fine. And trust me, I have an abnormally high tolerance for pain."

I giggled at my joke. Then I felt it, a presence. And it was angry. I quickly realized it was Anastase and he knew what I had just done. I concentrated as hard as I could to stop him. I told Justin I was going to take a shower and got off of the bed.

I headed to my bathroom and closed the door as I heard Justin move around in my room. I sensed he was putting my room back in order and getting dressed so he could head out. He was concerned that he'd acted too fast, even though he had let me make the first move. I'd have to reassure him that I was fine and let him know that he had no reason to feel any guilt.

I draped a towel over myself, sat down on the fluffy rug and concentrated on Anastase. I knew I could reach him just as easily as he could reach me and I was immediately in his mind. There was so much rage. I was careful as to what I was about to do.

"How dare you, you harlot? I told you that you were mine and yet you dared to bed another man, and a mortal to boot. Have you no shame, no decency?" He yelled at me.

"I am not yours and I do as I please," I said quietly.

"No! You belong to me and I will not stand for your actions!"

I breathed deeply for a moment and put a mental shell around myself so that he couldn't touch me. It must have worked, because he yelled in outrage. The potion was working to my favor again.

"You do not own me, Anastase. I'll see that you never touch me again."

He gave a maniacal laugh. "You honestly think that you can stop me? Do you realize the extremes I have gone to in order to be with you? What I have given up? There is no going back and you will be mine."

I shot out my power and I heard him cry out in pain. The power vibrated through me. I shut down our connection before he was able to rebound on me. I sped through the shower with vampire speed and found Justin on my bed waiting for me. I walked by the bed toward my closet. His hand whipped out to yank off my towel. He moved pretty fast for a mortal. I pulled away from him before he could get his hands on me, or I wouldn't be going to work on time tonight.

"Are you feeling okay?" He settled back on the foot of my bed.

"I'm fine, just like I was twenty minutes ago," I replied and got my butt popped by the towel.

He mumbled, "Smarty".

I wiggled my butt at him then grabbed some clothes for tonight.

"Let this be the last time we discuss this. I'm fine and what we did didn't hurt me at all. You didn't move too fast and I was in good enough shape to keep up with you. I'm well enough that I don't even feel like I was sick."

"What happened exactly?" He fiddled with the towel.

I got dressed as I explained.

"I have a blood illness. Perseus has it too. It causes us to have odd reactions to certain things and we become weak when we don't take care of ourselves. You and I haven't known each other long enough for me to explain things and there's much more to tell you. We'll have to take the time to really get to know each other."

I had my clothes on by this point and sat down at my antique vanity to deal with my wet hair and glowing face. Justin had a worried look on his face as he spoke.

"I feel bad about having sex with you after you were so ill. Perseus had me come over to watch over you so he could get your medication. This was our first time and you might not have been well enough for all that activity. You seem to be okay but you didn't seem that way last night. It's uncanny how quickly you recovered."

I turned to look at him. "I said we have a lot to learn about each other. I hope you still feel the same about me once you know all there is to know."

"You would have to be a very bad person for me to stop having feelings about you. I know you aren't evil. Just different."

"Can you please just let this moment be magical for me?"

I got up and kissed him with all the emotion I felt and hoped he understood.

We talked while I got ready and he walked me down a few blocks and then went home to finish processing the film he had started. It was nice that we had similar schedules. During our conversations, he told me he had always been a night person and took medicine to sleep on mornings he was too pent up to relax. He told me it started out with him being a baby with a mixed up schedule. I felt sorry for his mom. Unfortunately, she had passed away a long time ago and he had grown up as a foster child. His foster parents had died in a car wreck when he turned twenty, and he was alone again. But now we had each other. So he wasn't alone anymore.

I hummed to myself on my way to work. I felt like I was floating. Perseus was already there and I knew he had left the house early in order to leave me some mental privacy. I went into his office and kissed him on top of his head as a thank you.

"Well, I guess things went well?" He asked with a smirk on his gorgeous face.

"You know full well that it was amazing, although I was concerned about a couple of things. I figured you might be able to answer them."

I sat down on the edge of his desk, to make the conversation more private. He waved for me to go ahead.

"There was a small amount of blood afterward. Will it be like that every time? I also want to know if it'll be that amazing every time."

"Being a male, I'll do my best to answer those questions. Yes, sex is amazing, when done right. There are many ways to do it and I suggest you try them all," he said with a wide grin before he continued. "There's usually a small amount of blood when you're a virgin and I don't believe you'll experience that again. It would be horrible if each time was like your first time, but somehow we adjust."

"I know fluids are generated, so how do we do this without it being blood?"

"I honestly have no clue. Our tears are a mixture of blood and a small amount of saline that develops from our blood so maybe that's why. I've never asked anyone about that factor and am just happy that it isn't a problem. Can you imagine how disgusting that would be for both parties?"

Yes, it would be disgusting to have the vampires secrete blood when aroused. I understood his shudder.

"Well, that's all I have for you right now. Thank you for your honesty."

I kissed his forehead again and headed out of his office. He stopped me before I left the room. I looked back and he had the small glass vial from Bambara in his hand. He had attached it to another piece of leather and knew it would help to ward off Anastase for a little while longer. I had forgotten about the shell that had been snapped off of my neck and gladly slipped this replacement around my neck. Perseus winked at me. I whispered my thanks as I left his office.

I had started my usual duties when Danya walked over to me.

"You're beaming too well for someone who had to skip work. Were you really sick?"

"Yes, I was sick. But I'm better now. I'd neglected myself and it caught up to me. It's that blood illness I told you about last year. I got my medicine so I'm fine now. I also had some physical attention that worked wonders."

"Really? Would it have something to do with the gorgeous photographer that you've been seen with?"

"Yes, it would. He stayed with me and I woke up to a whole new world today."

"On my goodness, you had sex!"

Her mouth dropped open.

I was kind enough to reach over and shut her jaw for her as I nodded my head. It took her a minute to speak again.

"Uh, weren't you a virgin?"

"Yes, but not anymore," I smiled brightly.

"It's about bloody time!"

She hugged me and I laughed at the joke her comment was to me.

"Yes, I agree. It was perfect and not at all like I'd thought it would be. There was no awkwardness and I feel great."

I got back to work on my duties.

"I'm very happy for you. He better keep that smile on your face or I'll have to kick his heavenly ass all over the place."

It was nice how protective she was over me.

"I appreciate it. I hope he does as well. We have a lot to learn about each other and I hope he's still around after we get all our facts out."

"Well, keep me informed," she said as she patted me on the back. "I was headed to your brother's office to see what he wanted to do about the Renaissance Festival next week."

My face showed my shock.

"I had totally forgotten about that. Do we have a place already? Do I need to do that tomorrow?"

Being stalked by a black magic vampire had taken up too much of my mental abilities.

"I have a few to look over tonight and we could skip out early tomorrow to do that, if you want to help me," she offered as she headed to Perseus' office.

I finished up and headed back to his office. I was there just in time to see the same look of shock as he started shuffling papers. I was glad that we were more human than vampire or this wouldn't have affected us at all. Some vampires thought normal human circumstances were mundane, at best.

"Okay, we need to regroup. Between the new place and recent illnesses, I'm unprepared."

Danya stepped in and explained what needed to be done.

"I was called an hour ago as a reminder and they have three places for us to choose from. We can set up the usual mini bar and a table for the fortune telling. I told them Andromeda and I would be attending, like we did last year. They want an answer within two days on which location so the other two can be offered to the newcomers. I can check them out with Andromeda tomorrow if you can cover for us, and I'll fax them the final signup sheets afterward."

"Thank you, Danya. You are truly an asset to me. I mean, to us."

He floundered for a minute and it was adorable. She was the only woman in many years that could actually make my brother nervous. There was hope for them yet. Danya blushed.

"Okay, that's set up and we'll handle the rest as it comes. I have an idea of what drinks are needed and what we're allowed to serve. Andromeda can handle her setup and I'll just need a backup, if things get really busy here," Danya said as she recovered from her noticeable blush.

"I'll back you up and we can keep the rest here. I know what you need and the fortune telling is only for ambiance."

I smiled as I down played my part. I loved doing this event; it was close to how I'd grown up. I loved the street vendors and people in character.

I went back to my table and felt the confident vibes coming from Danya. It was wonderful to see her shine in those moments and I wanted so much happiness for her. I concentrated for a moment and felt the same admiration coming from Perseus and interrupted his train of thought.

"You need to be with someone like her, or just her, really." I mentally whispered.

"Butt out, sweetie."

I giggled and went back to my work.

The night went well and it ended much faster than I thought it would. I got everything ready and felt a little odd as I went to leave. I was a little dizzy and that fierce hunger showed its evil head. Perseus had stayed late to finalize the list of employees for Medusa's Manor. I wasn't going to interrupt him and knew I could hunt on my own.

I walked toward the cemetery and went to stand by my favorite tree there. There was a homeless man lying under it in a bed of leaves. I scanned his mind and saw no family, money or ambition. He was an alcoholic with no future and no drive to better himself. This would accomplish two things; I could feed off of him and give him the will to have a better life.

I swooped down on him before he had a chance to notice I was even there and I fed. He tasted of cheap booze and stale cigarettes, but I had to feed. I drank enough to assuage my hunger then placed my hand on his forehead. I instilled positive thoughts into his sleeping mind and then left him where I had found him. I felt satisfied with myself as I grabbed up my bag and headed back home. I had not killed the homeless man and it wasn't too hard to stop my thirst this time. Maybe I would be okay after all.

Perseus was in his study when I got home. I went up to my room for a shower and bed. I took my time in the shower since the water felt so refreshing against my skin. I increased the water pressure and stayed there until it started to turn cool. I rubbed off with a thick towel and climbed into bed without my even getting any clothes on. I could hear Perseus working in his office as I fell asleep.

I felt a pull again and knew that Anastase was behind it. I knew I was safely asleep in my bed so I didn't try to stop him. I decided to see what he had in mind before I broke the connection. I was set down softly on the deck of his old ship and he stood at the helm, tapping his foot. Thankfully, I wasn't naked in my dream. I was wearing the brown silk gown from the previous night. I leaned against the ropes and waited for him to speak. It didn't take long.

"I am still mad at you." He sounded like a five year old with a temper. "I do all these things to get to you and you throw your virginity away on a weak mortal. Have you no pity? No shame?"

"I am my own person and can do as I choose."

"Why him? I could have done more for you."

He was actually hurt.

"I don't have to justify my actions to you."

"Regardless, I have decided to forgive you," he said as he glanced at his clean-cut nails. "It was hard for me to calm down and you did give me quite a shock, but I'll manage. However, I warn you, I will not be as gracious the next time."

I laughed and he quickly advanced on me. He had his arms around me before the sound from my lips could even travel.

"Don't mock me. I have a great force behind me and I can obtain anything I want. You'd be wise to listen to my words." He stroked my cheek. "If you let one more man touch you, I will hurt all of your loved ones and then come after you."

He dove in to kiss me so fast that I had no time to block him. His lips were brutal and I felt his hunger for me. I wanted to push him off but my body stopped me, again. It wanted him just like it had before. I kissed him back with the same insatiable hunger. How could I do this with him? This was insanity.

He broke from my lips to take my throat. I broke the spell just before his teeth sunk into my flesh. I heard his chuckle as I woke up in my rumpled bed. I wondered why Perseus had not felt this. Maybe it was because I had gone willingly. I truly wished I knew the rules to this game so I could find a way around them. It took a long time for me to fall asleep again, but I had to keep up my strength.

* * * *

I woke up the next night and felt Justin's presence. He was in bed, at home, as he thought of me. I smiled and concentrated on him. He was lying in his bed, naked in his twisted sheets. I knew he had been awake most of the day. He had rushed out the prints from the shoot in the park and had been too pent up to sleep. He had wanted to come over to sleep with me but knew I would have been out cold by the time he arrived. I shot a mental image of myself to him. He gasped.

"Young lady, that is not decent."

He could speak out loud since no one was around him to question who he was talking to.

"I'm far from young and decent has nothing to do with it."

He smiled, "I wish I was there with you."

"You do?"

He nodded before he closed his eyes and concentrated on me. I could feel his hand sliding over me. It was as if the sheet at my waist had disappeared. I closed my eyes as well and let him touch me. It ran over my breasts and tweaked my nipples into tight buds. Then it tickled over my stomach and kept moving. I kicked back the sheet to allow him full access, visual and to touch. Decent be damned. I heard him chuckle and didn't care. I just hoped he would continue. He didn't disappoint me.

His hand roamed lower and I opened my legs to his exploring. Moments later I climaxed. It was amazing to feel this way and without him even being in the room with me. This was a side effect that I could definitely live with. As the waves subsided, I asked what he needed. He chuckled and I wondered if I could do the same for him. I thought about it and repeated the actions he took with me. And, like me, he climaxed in minutes. I waited for his breathing to slow down and smiled when he opened his eyes to me.

"Wow," was all he could manage.

"Anytime."

He smiled. "I'll be taking you up on that. It makes me forget how you're even doing this."

I retuned my own smile. "Same here."

We casually talked about what we were doing that night and he said he wanted to come by the bar before he came home tonight. I agreed and he said he would "call" me when he was on his way. I snickered since I knew it wouldn't be on my phone. We both had things to do so I broke contact and headed to work.

Perseus was there handling last minute details for the festival. Danya seemed anxious and I saw she planned to see Thomãs. She had texted with him for a few days and he'd planned to see her tonight when he brought the trunk by. He would be busy for a few days and wanted to meet her before the festival was over. She was nervous to see him tonight, even if it would be business related. The next time they could spend time together seemed far away and I felt weird about it but couldn't put my finger on why. I would have to mark it down as wanting her to be with Perseus and not some stranger in town.

Chapter Twelve

We had a slow night, so I easily picked up the vibes from Danya when Thomãs came in the door. He nodded at her as she headed to get Perseus. The three of them headed back out the front door but I caught Thomãs watching me before it closed behind them. I was curious as to why he frowned but was distracted by someone at the bar, so I got the customer a drink while Danya was outside. I stayed behind the bar until she came back in and Perseus told Thomãs to put the trunk in the office. Perseus reached in his wallet for the cash and paid Thomãs before the trunk even came into the building. I saw it as he wheeled it in with a hand truck and it was indeed perfect for the bar. I nodded at Perseus as he went to direct Thomãs where to leave it.

Danya came behind the bar and smiled at my approval of the trunk. We served a couple more drinks before I felt Justin call to me. Danya wondered why I looked happy all of a sudden, so I told her Justin was headed to see me. Thomãs sat at the bar with Danya as I went back to my table, and I felt Justin come in just as I was putting my things up.

I sensed he was tired but happy after he'd been paid well for the shoot he'd done. He'd been glad that he'd been able to complete his shoot and be with me without losing anything. I hugged him tight as he walked up and he chuckled into my ear.

"Whatcha doing later, little girl?"

"I'm taking a man home to my bed."

He nodded. "I think that's a brilliant idea."

We both laughed and I asked if he was thirsty. He nodded so I went to the bar to fix him something as he sat at my table.

Danya whispered to Thomãs as she leaned over the bar toward him. She practically shoved her push up bra in his face. Poor guy. Actually, poor Perseus, for not taking what this woman had offered to him. She winked at me as I walked around her and started fixing a strong Irish coffee with a dollop of whip cream on top.

I felt Thomãs' eyes on me as I walked back around the bar toward Justin. He turned to see where I was going. I heard him ask Danya who was with me. She answered and went back to discussing the festival in an excited voice.

I handed the warm drink over to Justin. He sipped at it and nodded before he put it down. I started laughing and couldn't stop myself; he had a dot of whip cream on his nose. He didn't know about it and made faces at me. I leaned over and licked it off the tip of his nose. He understood at that point and got turned on at the same time.

The laughter stopped as his eyes darkened and he took my hand. I watched him down the contents of the coffee before he pulled me toward the back corner of the bar. There was a small bathroom back past my brother's office and he pulled me inside. He had the door locked and me up on the sink in no time. I really liked how fast he worked.

He slipped one hand up the back of my shirt as the other bunched up my skirt at my thighs. He was happy to notice that I hadn't worn any undergarments and he took full advantage of it. I gripped the sink sides when I heard a pounding on the door.

I heard Justin say a gruff, "Occupied" as his hands roamed over me.

The pound sounded again and I heard Justin sigh. Someone really needed to be in here, so I jumped down and straightened my skirt by the time the door was unlocked. As the door opened I looked right into Thomãs' eyes. He was nervous. He shuffled by me as I heard him mumble something but I walked out just as the door was shut in my face.

"He must not be feeling well. Did you see his face? Something was eating at him for sure," Justin commented as he ushered me back up front.

I got back to my table and talked to Justin as Thomãs hurried by us. He headed to the bar and made his excuses to Danya, and waved over his head as he left. I guess he had gotten sick and needed to leave.

I talked to Justin while we closed up and he walked me home, hand in hand, as we learned more about each other. I could see him as a cute little boy with a crazy way of life. He was lucky to have had a foster parent who home schooled him after she got off work everyday. He had been hungry for an education but had a hard time making it to school with his days and nights so messed up because of his insomnia.

I let us into my house and walked him upstairs. I had offered him food but he said that wasn't what he needed. I could only agree with that. The conversations we had were great but I was still in limbo after we were interrupted in the bathroom. We had some business to finish.

Justin, not being one to waste time, simply said, "Make love with me."

I nodded in agreement.

I leaned forward to kiss him. His hands slid up my gaping shirt. I was already aching for him and we had barely even touched each other. He squeezed both of my nipples, switching from one to the other. I opened my mouth for his tongue and let him inside. We kissed and touched for several minutes, until it wasn't enough.

He yanked the shirt over my head before he threw it onto the floor. I used a little too much speed as I unbuttoned his shirt but he was too absorbed in my breasts to even notice. My palms grazed his tight nipples as he dove at mine again. I would never get enough of his touch on my skin.

His magic fingers worked their way up my skirt as I lay sprawled across his lap. I wanted his fingers inside of me. Then I felt something, something not right. But I ignored it as he slowly rubbed my clit. I threw my head back and offered myself to him.

He growled as he yanked down his pants. How could being with a vampire be better than this? I heard a rip and knew he had gotten another condom out but I wasn't about to tell him it wasn't needed. I gasped as I felt him position himself, and he slowly entered me. My world tilted.

Searing pain shot through my skull. I screamed. Justin stopped and hovered above me in fear. My cry had sounded feral. He knew something was wrong. I clasped my hands to my head, dug my nails into my skull. I was mute from the pain.

It was Anastase. He knew what I was doing and had kept his word. I had to get Justin out of here. But the pain was too intense to move. I felt Anastase as he drew near and knew he was furious with me for letting Justin touch me again.

I moaned, "Justin, please, get out of here."

"No, what's wrong? I'm calling your brother."

He reached for my discarded phone when black smoke filled the room. Anastase formed at the foot of the bed and I couldn't get Justin out in time.

I screamed, "No!"

Anastase simply laughed as he fully transformed into his modern self. Justin jumped when he saw a man standing there.

"What the hell?" That was all Justin could manage as the blonde man looked him over.

"Yes, what the hell, indeed," Anastase said with a sinister smile on his face. The pain decreased enough for me to be able to talk.

"Anastase, please let him leave. He doesn't know," I pleaded with Anastase.

"He doesn't know? You didn't tell him what we are? Is he nothing more than a plaything? You were about to bed him again, after I expressly forbid you to do so," Anastase said as he came toward me.

Justin got up to stand between Anastase and I but was knocked across the room by a simple flick of Anastase's wrist. Justin was shocked but got up and walked slowly toward me.

"Andromeda, what's going on? Who is this psycho?" Justin asked.

He intended to yank me away from Anastase, but I knew Anastase wouldn't allow it.

"Justin, stay where you are. This man will kill you without any thought whatsoever. I mean it, Justin."

He finally listened to me.

"Yes, Justin, listen to the psycho because he will kill you," Anastase said with a smile on his face. Then to me, he said, "Justin wants to know what's going on, so why don't we tell him?" His hand reached for my hair. I tried to shrink away but he grabbed my arm before I could move.

"Anastase, you and I can settle this alone. Just let him go. He has no idea who you are or what we're capable of. Just let him walk away."

I saw his anger as it burned in his eyes. He sauntered to the mattress and pulled me into his arms while Justin stood transfixed.

"Justin, please don't move."

Justin nodded since he knew this man was dangerous. I shot a message to Justin that this man was out of his mind and capable of anything. I wanted Justin to stay as still as possible so I could try to diffuse the situation before either of us got hurt. I wanted to compel him into a trance. Anastase sensed what I tried to do and laughed.

"Well, isn't this interesting. I knew I would find you like this but this isn't how I thought it would play out. I'm amused. I had wanted to tear this mortal apart and then have wild sex over his bloody remains."

"No," I said as Anastase's hand clutched my throat.

"Enough."

I concentrated on Justin's eyes enough to try and compel him into staying where he was, but he was in shock so it didn't affect him as much as it should have. I hoped that what I could do would be enough to save his life.

Anastase laughed low in his chest at the knowledge of what I'd done.

He whispered, "This changes nothing."

He leaned down to take my lips. I was powerless to stop his hands on my body. The guilt outweighed the lust. I couldn't see Justin's face but I felt his pain at seeing me in another man's arms.

Anastase quickly moved to my throat and I knew his intentions before the teeth ripped my flesh. I screamed at the pain in my head as I tried to stop him. Justin thought I had cried from the pain in my neck. He tried to shake himself loose of the compulsion. He lunged just as Perseus busted through the bedroom door and ran at Anastase. It was just enough of a distraction to push myself away from Anastase. I landed on the floor by the head of the bed and watched as Anastase threw both men off of him. Perseus landed on his feet but Justin's body crashed through my closet door. I felt Justin's pain as he tried to get up and knew he had been seriously hurt. Anastase looked at me and smiled before he turned into black smoke. Perseus tried to come at him again but went through the smoke and stopped quickly enough to keep himself from smashing my bed. Anastase was gone.

I went to Justin as Perseus surveyed the damage. I slipped my robe on as I pulled Justin up and heard his moan at the pain of just my gentle my touch. After I quickly assessed him, I found his left shoulder had been dislocated and he had obtained several abrasions from the splintered door.

"This is going to hurt," is all I said as I set his shoulder back to normal.

He didn't even yell. He looked at me with new eyes and stayed quiet. It was all new and fearsome for him to digest all at once. I sighed. The moment had come. I would have to tell him what I was and see how he'd take it.

I looked at Perseus and saw him shake his head, still against what I was about to do. But I didn't care anymore.

I helped Justin back to the side of the bed and said to my brother, "I have to do this. I won't curse this relationship with more deceit."

I knew he was not happy, but he knew not to argue with me, especially not now, and not about this. I sat down next to Justin, wrapped my coverlet around his body, and looked into his dazed eyes.

"You have some decisions to make. I can tell you what really happened or I can erase your memory and walk out of your life forever. Think carefully before you answer."

I sat there for a few moments and told myself that I'd be okay, that I wanted to be with this man, but not if he feared me. It would never work if he did. I had too many ethics in me yet to just compel him and live with the guilt for the rest of my life. He still hadn't said anything, but I felt sadness in the room. I knew then what his choice was. Feeling numb, I began to get up when I felt Justin's hand grasp mine. I looked back at him as he pulled me back onto the mattress.

"Tell me everything."

I felt joy and hope that this wonderful man accepted me for what I was. Perseus exhaled loudly and sat down. He didn't want to be a part of this, but his thoughts told me he had decided to be there for moral support, just in case Justin decided to reject me yet.

So, I told him my tale, all of it. I explained about the potion I'd taken and why, plus the side effects. He was a brave man and took in all the information I gave him. And never once did he let go of my hand. Perseus seemed to be in awe by the time I had finished, and looked at me with unexplained tenderness. In that moment, my dear brother knew that love was strong enough to conquer our immortal curse. After seeing that, Perseus approved and wanted me to be happy. I sent him the image of Danya in her underwear and his smile widened. He nodded at me as I waited for Justin to speak.

Finally, Justin spoke up. "Well, I told you that you'd have to be a bad person for me to leave your side. And I stand by what I said. You're an amazing woman, no matter what happened to you."

I believed what he said as his heart and mind had opened up to me. It was almost too much to take.

"I'm hurt that you didn't tell me the truth the first night that I sat with you at work, but I understand that normal people don't process this kind of information very well. However, to be with you, I'll deal with my injured pride and just move forward. I can get past this."

"Are you sure?"

His answer was a tender kiss on my lips. I pulled him closer, forgetting his injured shoulder. I kissed him with all the emotion that I felt, heedless of my brother who stood by. Perseus would have to get used to public displays of affection from us. He groaned at my mental comment, picked up the shattered pieces of my closet door, and excused himself from the room.

We had a couple of hours of the morning to answer each other's questions and then I would need to sleep. The event had been a strain on both of us. We snuggled back into my bed and talked until sleep took us both.

I woke up in Justin's arms and smiled while he slept. I was laying between his legs with my head on his ribcage. We had come to this position during the wee morning hours, so I knew my weight wouldn't disturb his aching shoulder. He had declined any pain killers I offered, so instead I massaged it with my cool marble hands until the muscles had eased up.

I had too many things on my mind to sleep, so I left the bed without waking him. I grabbed up my phone and went downstairs.

Perseus was getting ready for work so I had a small amount of time to explain what was needed.

Bambara had to be told what had happened; she'd only gotten glimpses. Anastase's power had come from someone with voodoo power and it blocked her out as well. To have any chance of beating him, we'd have to take away his magic source. Bambara would see what she could do on her end. I had just one request for her, that Justin be protected as well. After finishing discussing Justin, she agreed that she'd send me a talisman for him. I only hoped Justin would wear it so I wouldn't have to compel him to do so. Justin and I had agreed during the night that we were to be honest with each other and that I wouldn't compel him unless necessary. I had to respect this. He also said that I could drink his blood if needed. I worried about this since my hunger had been too great after the potion had taken affect. I didn't want to harm him, and I'd rather not take any chances with him. Perseus had once told me that drinking from someone during sex was even more thrilling than sex alone. I was excited and nervous to test that theory when Justin was out of immediate danger.

Perseus came down as I finished my call. I quickly briefed him about what Bambara had said before making an omelet from the dried goods we had in the pantry. It would have to suffice. I finished quickly and headed upstairs just as Justin woke up. I sat on the bed and massaged his shoulder as he quietly ate his meal.

"I'm sorry that it isn't top quality, but with us being vampires we don't keep perishable food around here. It would only spoil."

He nodded over his almost empty plate.

"I understand, and it's fine. Stop being uncomfortable. This is going to take some adjusting on both of our parts. Besides, bachelors are used to instant meals." He smiled as he swallowed the last bite and got up.

God, he was gorgeous. Justin walking around in his boxer briefs was one of the most beautiful things I'd ever seen in my long life. He headed downstairs to wash his dishes. I remade the bed with fresh linens and was in the shower by the time he came back upstairs.

He shared the shower with me and washed my hair, which no man had done since I was six. Sadly, we knew there would be no sex until I was released from Anastase's clutches, so the shower ended with cold water and a bittersweet feeling.

We both dressed and separated as I headed to work and he went home to check on the details of his next shoot. At work I spent most of the day arranging the final things for the festival with Danya. At the end of the day I gave Perseus the details and headed home.

I spent the first half of my night with Justin as we roamed the streets with his camera. He looked for local shots to shoot in black and white for a gallery in town. I showed him things as seen through my vampire eyes. He was eager to learn more about my world.

I explained the problem with being captured by normal 35 mm film. He laughed as he realized why the pictures of me had not developed correctly. I showed him that he could take some with his more advanced digital camera and he took several shots of me as we wandered the streets. I even let him take one of me as my eyes glowed in the darkness like a cat's. He promised he would obscure my form so no one could figure out that it was me.

I had gotten the amulet Bambara over-nighted and gave it to Justin with his promise not to take it off until all of this mess was over. It came with a note from her that explained she had investigated Anastase's power source and would give us details later.

My thoughts of Bambara made me consider all of the things that had happened and how it could involve Justin. I suddenly recalled my visions of him and realized two had already come to fruition. My visions showed when we had walked around holding hands and he had kissed me at my door, and when we'd been about to have sex in my room just as Anastase had interrupted us, both had already passed. I kept these realizations to myself and tried to quiet the fear in my mind. I couldn't let him die. That one had to be false.

He kissed me at my front door and I shut myself in as I fought the stirrings of a strong hunger for fresh blood. I had called the evening short, as the need had gotten stronger and stronger, not wanting for him to be my prey. I was honest enough to tell him that I had to feed, but not at the depth of how bad it was. I silently waited for him to leave the house and then concentrated on my next prey.

I quickly found one and was on my way within seconds of his Mustang leaving the sidewalk. The hunger was so strong that by the time I got there I had to force myself not to drain the woman I fed on. It was a very close call and I tried not to feel the guilt that was weighing on me as I closed her neck before I had laid her on the ground.

I went home and started working on the remaining garments that Danya and I would wear to the festival. We had the essential pieces but I wanted to give her something different to wear each night. It helped to take my mind off of the lady I had almost killed and focused it onto something positive for my best friend.

The outfits were a combination of gypsy and pirate. They would be easy to work in plus they had a sexy edge. I knew Perseus would have a hard time keeping his eyes off of her. Working in vampire speed, I finished four outfits by the time I felt sleep coming on. I packed the three for Danya in a gift bag and got into bed before I was too tired to move.

* * * *

I gave Danya her clothes at work on Monday night. We took a break when things slowed down and went into Perseus' empty office for her to try them on. The first outfit was red and cream striped leggings with a blood red hip scarf and cream peasant blouse. The second outfit was brown leggings with a matching brown pirate shirt and I borrowed the red hip scarf to give it a splash of color. The third one was the sexiest and I knew Perseus wouldn't be able to ignore her in this one. I was thrilled to see how giddy she was over how great she would look in them. I felt Perseus as he drove toward the bar and knew he would be there in time for him to see what I had made.

The third outfit had a ragged edge black skirt made of transparent muslin. It was paired with a muted purple corset that had black satin laces. It made her look dark and statuesque. I held up a finger to her as I had stuck my head out of the office door. She giggled as I called Perseus to join us.

I patiently waited and had put on my poker face by the time he came through the door. He stopped short, just in front of me and had stared at Danya. There was a hunger in his eyes that I now knew very well because I looked at Justin the same way.

Clearing my throat, I said, "What do you think? I made it for the festival and had to make sure it fit. Is it too sexy?"

Danya just stared at him, daring him to say something negative. Instead he cleared his own throat and spoke to me without taking his eyes off of Danya.

"No, she looks delicious."

She did her part as she had thanked him and then turned so he could get a view of the whole outfit. I folded the other two outfits but he stopped me before they were put back in the bag.

"Danya, show me what else you have."

I was very happy to hand them over to her across the desk and excused myself as they talked. Maybe he was getting smart.

I finished the rest of my night as I usually did and never asked Danya what had happened. I did, however, see the looks they passed each other during the remainder of the shift.

Her mind had kept playing the brief scene over and over again. He had taken the clothes from her and had placed them back in the bag but had stopped just inches from her face. He had placed his hand over hers and she had held her breath as she had waited. But before he could do anything else he had mentally shaken himself and stepped away.

The next three days were filled with final decisions over the festival and a few stolen moments with Justin. He had been accepted in the gallery so he used his spare time to get enough material to fill his section of the display. I was so happy for him, even if I did miss waking up to him each morning.

We had everything ready when Friday came and Danya met me at the house wearing the cream and red outfit that I made for her. She chatted non-stop as we loaded the boxes into my Jaguar and headed toward River Street. We set up our spot in fifteen minutes and our first customers arrived not more than five minutes later.

We stayed busy all night. At closing time we dropped the money off at the bank depository and got Danya off toward her apartment. I offered for her to stay with us during the festival, but she was adamant about not spending the night unless it was for more pleasurable circumstances. I knew she was talking about Perseus, but that she was too stubborn for her own good and my brother was too blind. One day I would lock them in a room together. Maybe that would solve everything.

Chapter Thirteen

I fed early in the night and let Justin in about ten minutes after I finished my shower. He came up and sat with me as I got ready before Danya showed up. It was hard not jumping the man as I changed clothes. The hum of the prostitute's blood I had drunk still pumped through my veins. The images of her sexual acts I got while drinking her blood turned me on instantly. But I was good and left her some cash and a smile on her face before heading out of her hotel room. The few passionate kisses from Justin as I dressed weren't enough. But Justin did love the outfits I had made. I had on black leggings, a burgundy peasant blouse and a white hip scarf on with black knee high leather boots. A matching white scarf was in my hair and large silver hoop earrings glinted from my ears.

He kept running his hand over my butt every time I walked near him; at least I knew he still desired me after knowing what I am. Perseus had thought Justin would run hysterically from the house when Anastase left, but Justin had made up his mind to stick this out. However, despite the excitement I felt over the costume, and Justin, and the festival, I knew I would have to deal with Anastase soon, and the waiting was wearing my nerves thin.

Danya pulled up outside, and I kissed Justin goodbye, for several minutes, before he walked me down. Once we were on our way we were busy again and barely took a break to grab a few beignets for a much needed sugar rush. I craved blood again but I knew the pastries didn't come in O positive. I had hidden a blood bag in my purse before I left, and covered it in aluminum, so no one would recognize what it was. I devoured it while Danya had gotten our treats. The cravings came more frequently and were harder to deal with now that I had taken another dose. I'd have to be more prepared for the next few days.

I wondered if I needed a consort that I could keep handy for just these difficult moments. Perseus had seen those images in my mind and had sent one of Angelica to me as my answer. But I

quickly shook the thought from my mind. I didn't want that for
her. I just couldn't live my life that way. People were not to be
used as crutches or cattle, no matter what other vampires said.
Perseus was amused by this but understood.

Danya was a little depressed that she hadn't seen Thomãs in a
while, but he was supposed to hang out with her tomorrow before
taking her back home. She had debated having sex with him since
it had been awhile. Plus she'd been so turned on by Perseus lately
that she needed a little action. I once again silently hoped it
wouldn't work out with Thomãs so she could try to get closer to
Perseus.

The long night finally finished and we headed back to my
house. I hugged her good night and then headed off to hunt. I
drank two homeless people this time and yet still needed more.
This looked grim. I hunted for a third and almost emptied him as
well. I then headed back to my home in order to wash the stench
off of my body. I had left all three of them with money and food to
fight my ever growing guilt.

After my steamy shower I felt overwhelmingly tired so I
crawled under my covers after tossing on a thin silk chemise. I
didn't even have the strength to refasten the leather cord that had
slipped from my neck while washing my hair. The feel of it on my
skin made me feel better. But I couldn't relax, and realized that I
needed more blood to take with me tomorrow. Walking to the
kitchen, I wrapped four aluminum blood bags and had them ready
to place in my hobo bag for tomorrow. The night was balmy but
with a delicate breeze, so I went onto the balcony for a moment
before heading back to the bathroom for my necklace. Taking one
final inhale, I smelled something intoxicating. Too intoxicating. I
smelled the air once more and pinpointed it as it came toward the
house. My mouth watered and I had to grip the banister to stop
myself from jumping down to devour whatever came my way.
Then I saw it, or rather him, with his glowing eyes. Anastase. He
stood under the tree in front of my house. He wore a black leather
jacket over his bare chest and dark wash jeans tucked into black
leather boots.

It was as if I hadn't fed in days. He must have done something
for me to crave his blood this badly. Who cared if it was the one
poisonous snake that would most certainly bite me? He smelled

like lust, power, darkness, and strength, all at once. He bowed to me as he caught my gaze. I wondered what the snake would do next, and seeming to hear my thoughts, the very next moment he stood on the other side of the balcony. I stepped back until my back rested against the iron railing and held onto the sides as I waited for him to strike. Putting a hand to my neck, I then realized I was so exhausted I'd forgotten to put the vial back around my throat when I finished the shower.

I had no wish to fight him and didn't have the strength, even if I desperately wanted to. He stepped within one foot of my leaning body and smiled. I wondered if Perseus would know Anastase was here; if he would burst out here at any moment. Anastase slowly shook his head at my unasked questions. He closed his eyes and showed me a mental image of Perseus at work, with papers all around him. Perseus would not be coming home tonight.

Anastase inhaled deeply and smelled my hunger for his blood and silently laughed as he reached inside his jacket. I leaned further over the railing, knowing I could jump if I had to. But before I could, he used a razor sharp nail to cut an X into the thin skin over his breastbone. I smelled that dark liquid and my knees buckled as it dripped down the smooth surface of his chest. It overwhelmed me.

He crooned to me, "You know you want a taste. And there is nothing wrong with that. You are so thirsty."

I involuntarily leaned toward his blood wet chest as he slipped the supple leather jacket off his shoulders. It hit the floor with a thud that was like a drum in my ears. I wanted his blood so badly. I ached for it. The devil's eyes drew my attention as they looked straight into mine. I knew nothing but him at that moment. My body wanted to give into him completely. My mind kept shouting at me, but I muffled out the noise as I leaned my face down toward his blood offering.

I moaned when my tongue touched the dark substance. It put my senses over the edge. I drank from the deep center of the wound and felt his hands in my hair as he held me against that sinful spot. I drank like a newborn and tasted his desire for me as it mingled with the dreams he had for us. It was his fantasy world for us. I saw how he felt when he had changed me, his loss as he had discovered I had been missing and the joy when he had found me again. It seemed so genuine it was hard to disbelieve he could feel such things.

I drank until I felt it pull directly from his heart. A moan sounded deep in his chest as I sapped his strength with my hunger. I had to hold him up as I took everything he had to offer me. The rush of desire ran rampant as I wanted to take him inside of me, his blood warm on my tongue.

But then I saw it, the one thing that made me pull back. It was the picture of what had happened to my family. I knew he had no remorse for that crime and had done it only to meet his selfish needs. And yet here I was, welcoming him. My brain clicked and I flew away from him before he passed out on my stone balcony.

I turned and ran as if a demon was on my tail. I needed to escape what I had just done. How could I? What did this man have over me that he could make me forget who I am? What had become of me? Had I lost my mind or worse, my soul?

I ran until I ended up at the wildlife park. My soul ached more than my body ever could as I found a quiet grassy spot and forced myself to stop and when I did, my actions caught up to me. I fell to the ground and cried. I cried for the past life that had been taken away from me. I cried for the lives that had been affected since that terrible day, long ago. I cried for the way that I had betrayed myself. I cried for what I knew that I had to do. I had to kill Anastase if I was ever to get out of this with my very sanity. I cried until there was nothing left in me.

After the bloody tears were wiped away and I stopped shaking with my self-hate, I got up. I had to go home. I couldn't ignore what had happened there. I couldn't let him keep me from my sanctum, my home. I had to go back and fix the mess that had become my life. I took my time going home, using that time to think over what I needed to do when I got there.

I saw the light on in Perseus' office and readied myself for this confession. I walked in the door and he was bent over the stack of papers in his hands. A quick search of his mind showed that things seemed to be okay. He was ignorant as to what had happened. I sat down in his supple leather chair and waited for him to look up from his papers.

"Someone was out all night," he said as he kept shuffling papers. He still hadn't looked up.

"Yes. I need to talk to you about that." But my voice had never sounded so alien to my ears. It was so quiet. So broken.

That got his full attention, and I told him what I had done. He was patient and didn't interrupt. When I finished, he did nothing but continue to stare at me.

"Go ahead and say what you're thinking," I said to him when I was done.

He didn't fuss like I thought he would. He pointed out the consequences of being anywhere near Anastase, plus the blood lust causing more problems. He made me promise to tell him when I was in dire need again and to make sure that I wasn't alone all of the time. And that was all. I hugged Perseus as I headed to my room to get ready. Danya would be here in about fifteen minutes.

I had showered, changed and even checked in with Justin by the time Danya pulled up. She was wearing the purple corset outfit I made and had her hair in braids wrapped around her head in a coil. It left her neck exposed and her shoulders naked. It was very sexy. I was wearing a similar outfit that was all black with knee high boots. We were quite a pair.

Perseus had come down to see us off. He practically salivated as he appraised Danya's finished appearance. When he hugged her good bye, he had placed a soft kiss under her ear. She blushed but didn't look away from his intense gaze. I smiled and got us on our way.

As the night progressed, we had a couple of drunks to dismiss but they went quietly enough. By around 1 a.m. Danya got a text that Thomãs was on his way. When she asked if that was okay, I told her that was fine by me since we had to start closing down by 2 a.m. Justin had his gallery showing while we had worked and would be by to give me the details once he was done taking everything back down. I sensed that he had done well and that the picture of me dancing under a willow tree had sold. I was very proud of the work he had done.

Sometime after 2 a.m. we were taking boxes back to the car. We had sold out of almost everything, so there wasn't much to worry over. The bar supplies fit snuggly in my trunk. Thomãs drove up next to us in the parking lot and asked Danya to go for a walk. I told her to call me if she needed me then I headed off to hunt before Justin showed up.

I was quick with my prey. I had fewer cravings after the ingestion of Anastase's enticing blood. I was back at my car when I saw the Mustang pull up beside me. I glanced around and Thomãs' truck was still in the lot. Apparently Danya and Thomãs were still walking around.

Justin and I took our own little walk hand in hand down Bay Street for a little while. Most of the festival people were headed out and there was a lot of traffic on the streets. We meandered over to a street vendor that was still open and got two cups of iced coffee before we headed back to the vehicles.

As we walked away, it hit me. It was intense. I dropped my coffee on the sidewalk and gasped in pain. Something was wrong. I realized then that it was the pain that came from Anastase's dark power. Justin heard me utter Anastase's name and whirled around to see if there was a threat nearby. He saw nothing, but threw away his own coffee and got me back to the parking lot.

By the time we reached the car I heard it. Someone was calling my name but it was too faint to make out whom it was. I was powerless to resist it. I leapt away from the fender of the Mustang and started to follow the voice, sensing dread. I focused my energy on tracking the source as I worked through the pain in my skull. It took me back down to River Street as it became louder in my head. I was then able to make out who it was. It was Danya and she was in pain. I grabbed Justin's hand and pulled him to where she was whispering my name. She was lying on the embankment at the waterline, covered in her own blood. It was just like my vision. *Oh my God.*

Her heartbeat was erratic. She had lost a large amount of blood and the smell of it was in the air. It took everything in me to remember that this was my best friend and not my prey. I called out to Perseus and started assessing Danya's injuries. She had a gaping hole in her neck that she was weakly applying pressure to. I knew without help she would bleed to death soon.

I could smell a vampire's scent and recognized it as Jean Luc's. Breathing in deeper, I smelled a bit of Giselle's and Thomãs' as well. She had been ambushed. I had Justin keep pressure on the wound using my hip scarf. I knew Perseus would be here in a moment. I told her not to talk, and she just looked at me with fear in her eyes.

I put my hands on each side of her blood-covered face and concentrated on what had happened. Thomãs had brought her out here to be attacked by Jean Luc and had left her to her fate. Damn that man! He had been working for them the whole time. They had used her to get to me. He had warned me that this would happen. I had failed to protect my best friend.

I whispered, "I'm sorry" to Danya as I pulled more images from her mind.

She had been kissing Thomãs when Jean Luc and Giselle had appeared. He had ripped her from Thomãs' arms and had fed off of her as Thomãs walked away. Giselle sat back and watched as Jean Luc drank her blood until she had passed out. Danya had woken back up as he was kissing Giselle, and then she took her turn at Danya. But Jean Luc still wanted to play with this gorgeous woman so he had bitten his wrist to drink and poured his own blood directly into Danya's mouth as Giselle held her down. Jean Luc had laughed as Giselle ripped the hole in Danya's neck. Jean Luc and Giselle made out as they licked Danya's blood off each other.

They had thought that Giselle had emptied her of Jean Luc's vampiric blood, but they hadn't. Danya's body had been drained to nothing but had absorbed enough of Jean Luc's blood that she had started the change. I gasped at what I saw but there was nothing I could do to stop it. Those monsters thought she was dead and had walked away from her body. But they were wrong. She wasn't dead. She only had a few hours before her body would be transformed forever. I knew the look in Danya's eyes. She had guessed at my true way of life many years ago but had never wanted to speak the words and she was afraid of what had happened, what was going to happen, and what she would be.

Perseus got there as I let go of Danya's face. I apologized to her over and over again. Justin just looked at me, wondering. I shook my head at his unasked question, knowing it was too late. He let go of her neck and realized there was no more blood coming out of the fatal wound. I noticed with my vampire eyes that it had started to close, a little at a time, as her body began to repair itself. She still didn't speak, and I knew she was trapped inside her body. I had been unconscious much of my time during my transformation; certainly not as aware as Danya was. Perseus could smell the same things I had and had started to put the pieces together. I sent him a fast paced version of what I had found out from her mind. He was enraged.

I bit my wrist and held it out to Danya. I knew this would help her heal faster. She was reluctant to take it, but I knew the moment she accepted it. She knew that she would have to live this way the rest of her immortal life. I held my wrist to her parted lips and squeezed the blood into her mouth. She was too weak to suck, but strong enough to at least gulp down what I fed to her. Justin stayed at my side and Perseus held Danya's hand as she finished drinking from me.

Then the spasms came. It was her body's last fight before it gave up and began to petrify. Perseus cried pink tears as he held her down to the blood soaked ground and straightened her clothes to cover any embarrassing evidence. All this time, Justin was by my side. He knew this could be his fate and yet he was there to witness my friend go through this horrid experience. He simply wrapped his arms around me as I saw the last spasm wrack Danya's body. She then stayed limp in my brother's arms.

Tomorrow night she would be one of us. We would have to teach her how to feed and help her transition her life as best we could. Knowing my friend, she would wake with a strong thirst for blood and a stronger need for the life of the man who had done this to her. And I vowed then that I would help her do that. I owed that to my best friend.

Perseus kissed her closed lids and held her close to his chest as he picked her up. He would take her to our home and clean her up. I held on to Justin as we walked back to the cars in silence. We drove back to our quiet house and went upstairs to help Perseus take Danya into the bathroom of his suite. I stripped her and bathed her as Justin went with Perseus to find clothes in my closet that would fit Danya. After a moment, Perseus came back with a red silk pajama set and I completed my task of bathing her. Perseus just stood in the door, saying nothing the entire time.

Once I finished, Perseus then carried her to his bed and tucked her into the freshly changed sheets. The savagery done to Danya had taken away my thirst for blood and replaced it with vile anger for the people responsible. All three of us sat a quiet vigil until sleep called to us all.

Perseus waved me away to bed as he became aware of dawn approaching, but I refused to leave the room. Justin persuaded me to move to the large suede sofa in the corner and we curled up to sleep there. Perseus climbed into the bed and curled up against Danya as he waited for her to wake up. She would have many questions when she woke up and we wanted to be here for her. We all slept and I wondered what the new day would bring for us all.

* * * *

I woke up first as dusk washed over the horizon. I stretched against Justin's body as he snored and I absorbed his warmth while I looked at the people in the room. I wondered how long it would take for Danya to open her new eyes to the world.

Perseus and Justin woke at the same time shortly after, but with different emotions. Justin was worried over what would happen next but knew we would handle it together. Perseus battled between anger for what had happened to Danya and worry over whether she'd accept us now. He had realized last night just how deeply he felt for her and feared that she'd reject him like Valentina had. If she walked away from him now, he'd be devastated. He squeezed her body to himself and waited.

I got up and poured Perseus and myself a glass of blood. He initially refused, but I forced him to take it since we needed to stay strong, which he knew to be true. I would see my brother exact his revenge on the ones who had committed this crime. As we finished with our blood we saw that Danya was coming back to us.

Her eyelashes fluttered as her fingers twitched on top of the covers. Perseus ran his hand over her hair and whispered soft words to her as Justin and I moved to the bedside. She finally opened her eyes. We could see them dilate as she observed her surroundings with her new, vampire eyes. She inhaled all the new

scents around her and started assimilating them. She looked up at
the faces around her.

I quickly left the room and got another glass of blood since I
knew Danya would need it soon. All newborns woke with a
tremendous thirst and it was best to alleviate it soon, in order to
keep them from striking the first blood source they encountered,
human or vampire. I saw her nostrils flare as I brought it close to
the bed. She sat up and reached for the blood instinctively. That
was a good sign. I knew of some newborns that went mad once
they realized what they were and starved themselves to death. I felt
more positive about the vibes coming from her and smiled at
Perseus' strained face. I knew this was so hard for him. I touched
his hand for a moment as she finished the contents of the large
glass. After handing it back to me she looked at all of us again and
I saw that familiar stubborn glow in her gleaming eyes.

I smiled at her. She nodded at me as she accepted her new life.
She had always been able to deal with whatever mortal life had
thrown at her and now she would do the same in her immortal one.
A single pink tear ran down my cheek as I patted her hand before I
set the glass aside. Perseus let out a long sigh; he'd been holding
his breath as he waited for Danya's decision. He hugged her
against his chest and she let him. Now that she had accepted her
future, we could move on to helping her adjust.

She had many questions for us, but started by asking the
simplest one.

"How were you guys changed?"

I explained it as briefly as possible and Perseus filled in the
parts that I had not seen.

"I knew something was unusual about you guys. I'd even
guessed at the supernatural. But I was afraid to say the words, so I
chose denial. You guys have had two years to set me straight. Did
you honestly think I'd hate you for something you had no control
over? You should've known me better than that."

Perseus knew he would have to tell her the full story, so he
went ahead and poured his heart out about Valentina and the
mistakes he had made with her. And after that, she understood.
That didn't mean she was less hurt, she just saw how he'd felt and
why he couldn't go through that pain again. She leaned back into
this chest and kissed him softly on the lips, accepting him in true

Danya fashion. I could've screamed for joy but I held back as we knew things were about to get worse.

She started getting back her images of all that had happened the night before and remained strong as we explained what changes had taken place. She even remembered how my brother had looked when he'd seen what had been done to her. Perseus and I took turns explaining the things she would need to know as a newborn and that she'd need to stick closely by our sides until she got the hang of it.

She'd have to decide on whether she wanted to stay at her apartment and how to hide her true nature to the people who lived there. Perseus offered for her to stay with us while she learned. She wanted very much to live here permanently, to share a room with Perseus, but wouldn't do so unless he wanted her as his mate. I agreed, but also knew it wouldn't take long before Perseus gave her just that.

She got up after a few hours of listening to us and asked the question that we had feared the past twenty-four hours.

"When were we going after those bastards?"

That was difficult to answer. I knew we'd have to destroy them but it'd be dangerous to attempt it with Danya being so new. She'd need to learn to defend herself plus get past her distraction with feeding before she could commit herself to this battle.

Perseus excused himself to call Bambara as I found clothes suitable for Danya to wear as she fed for the first time. Later on we could go by her apartment to get the things she'd need for the next few days. Running at a speed that was a blur to the human eye would be the first thing she'd learn. It'd be harder for her to learn how to smell her prey because it took more concentration for a new vampire.

Justin decided to go to the gallery to finish his business with them over the merchandise he'd sold. I'd miss him, but was glad that he wouldn't be around because it'd be more difficult for Danya to concentrate on her prey with human blood pounding so close to her. I had kissed him goodbye before we walked Danya to a deserted part of town to start honing her new skills.

Chapter Fourteen

It took a couple of nights for Danya to get comfortable with running and hunting down her prey. She agreed with us on only hunting down people that were bad for the community and that death should be considered only as a last resort. It would take a little longer for her to be able to compel someone, so we handled that part for her as she watched and learned. Her strength was also an issue. She had to learn how to hold her vampire strength back in order to remain normal in human eyes. She decided to stay at our place a few more days in order to keep up the appearance.

All in all, she only took a week off from work. During that time, we told people that she had gotten sick and just needed a few days to get over it. Everyone believed it and only noticed a few slight differences in her as she came back to work four days later. Her skin had stayed as tan as it was when she was human, but as a vampire she had more glow to her appearance. She seemed more defined. They thought she'd recovered well and the rest had done her some good.

Her new life style seemed to agree with her, and she embraced everything that she could. It was marvelous to see her push through this with courage. She even decided to sleep with Perseus at night, breaking her previous vow to herself. It warmed me to see him reach out to her each day, as they increased their bond. His walls crumbled down slowly and I hoped she'd be able to jump over the rubble of that wall very soon.

She was lethal in her hunting by the end of the week and could hide most of the signs of her super strength to outsiders. Anytime she slipped up she just used the excuse that she'd been working out with a trainer ever since she'd gotten sick. Her life melted into ours and it seemed like she'd always been there.

I had not had any visits from Anastase or his crew since the night I almost drank him dry. I wasn't sure if he was healing or if he was gathering up his resources for another attack; I hoped for the first. I kept him in the back of my thoughts as I focused on my new routine.

Then reality crashed in again.

One morning after work, Danya, Perseus and I had come home to see a long white box at the front door. I picked it up and was curious as to who'd sent something to us. I smelled flowers and the scent of the man who'd haunted me for centuries. I wanted to throw the box but refrained from doing that since Danya cautiously watched me. I sent her a look and she stepped closer. She had picked up on my body language and sensed something was wrong. She stood in front of me and prepared herself as I opened the white box.

Inside were two long stemmed roses. One rose was black and had no thorns while the other was deep red with thorns all along the length of the stem. Each had a white card attached to it. Perseus came up behind me as I read each card. The card for the black rose had my name scrawled on it and unfortunately the red rose was for Danya.

She slowly pulled out her red rose as if it were a lethal snake and snapped the card off. I opened my card and handed the box over to Perseus. I read mine first.

I will see you again soon, my love.

That meant he was coming for me. I felt the anger peel off of Danya as she threw the rose so far that it landed in a tree across the street. She flashed into Perseus' arms and stayed there until I took the box away from Perseus and grabbed the crushed note from the front step.

I caught another scent in the air. It was Jean Luc, and he was watching us from a distance. He was amused at the reaction Danya had given. She looked up at me with angry pink tears running down her face as she heard his laugh.

I enjoyed that night and am looking forward to another, very soon.

Perseus was livid. "That does it. He dies."

He took Danya inside, away from the eyes that watched her. I set everything down and went inside for a moment, only to come back out with a lighter and a metal wastebasket. Those eyes watched as I set the black rose and flower box into the basket, and then lit it. The box caught immediately. I pointed at it as it engulfed in flames and pointed out to where the eyes were stationed. This was a message and it was received. I was going to see them burn.

I went back into the house and sent an image to Perseus on what I'd done. He agreed and had gotten Danya to bed with a promise that she'd be rid of her demon very soon. She went into a troubled sleep that kept Perseus up most of the night. He held on to her and sang old gypsy songs as he fought her nightmares and vowed he'd never see her like this again.

* * * *

The next night we talked to Bambara and she'd come up with a couple of things that could help us fight Anastase and his crew. She knew who was behind Anastase's power, and how to stop him. She'd also be joining us for the battle. The logistics were all quickly worked out and we fed before going to bed with renewed feelings about what was to come.

We hadn't forgotten the grand opening and knew that we had to be in Louisiana that Friday. Work would be covered for us and we packed for a more positive couple of nights. I had hoped that this would take our strained minds off of the near future but it stayed in the back of our minds at every step.

We were set up in a large suite at Frank's hotel. Frank was slightly surprised that we had a newborn with us, but didn't ask any questions. Danya stayed in Perseus' room while I had one all to myself. We got dressed together, in my suite, and headed to a meeting with the new employees for a quick talk before we officially opened the doors. Everything looked great and everyone seemed to be in great spirits. The pep talk had everyone clapping as Perseus opened the door to the line that had formed outside. Frank had done a bit of advertising on his end and we were glad for his help.

We were to bring Bambara back home with us on Sunday and leave the new manager to take over on Medusa's Manor. Danya and I would supervise the first and second floors while Perseus greeted people at the front door with Angelica. Everyone knew what positions they were over and had their uniforms delivered two days ago. I had made togas for me, Angelica and Danya to wear. They were all short and white with gold cording laced around our mid sections. I had also found low-heeled gold gladiator sandals in all of our sizes. We'd end up looking like three muses by the time we fixed our hair and got dressed.

We had tried to talk Bambara into coming to opening night, but she claimed to be too old for such events. We argued with the mere fact that we were much older than her; she just laughed as she declined again.

Angelica looked beautiful as she greeted people coming in and quickly got people seated for dinner or directed them to the bars upstairs. Thankfully, Danya had learned that Perseus was not interested in Angelica. We didn't need any more tension. But what it did cause was a few dirty jokes about my love life that Justin wasn't ever to hear. Even though I missed him, I was kind of glad that he was at home sorting out the arrangements for his gallery exhibit.

The night went with only a few hitches until I sensed him come to the door. I mentally called to Perseus and Danya. Danya had gotten used to our mental abilities very quickly and wished she could have the same physic powers that we did, but at least we could use them to contact her. They were by my side at the hostess area when Anastase and Giselle walked in, arm in arm. Danya quietly hissed when she saw Giselle but kept herself still.

"What can I do for you?" Perseus tried to act cordial.

Anastase addressed Perseus. "We heard about your new place and wanted to see it for ourselves. It looks like you've received a large crowd for your first night."

"Yes, we're doing very well. Now that you've seen it for yourself, I'll let you get back to your evening." Perseus waved back toward the front door behind Anastase and Giselle.

Anastase and Giselle just looked at each other and then laughed.

"We've only seen the front entrance! Are we not allowed into your fine establishment?" He asked this a little more loudly so that people close to them would over hear it.

He was trying to push his limits in the public eye. I placed my hand on my brother's elbow.

"We can let them walk around for a minute. They'll be bored and leave in no time at all." I said this as I looked at Giselle, who already looked bored as she still clung to Anastase.

Anastase raked his eyes over me and smiled. "Beautiful as usual, my love, but I do prefer you in your gypsy attire."

I was thankful he didn't refer to my being nude the last time he had seen me. "Thank you, this goes with our theme. Now, the bar is behind me and one more is on the second floor where jazz music will be playing."

"What? No tour? I'm hurt," he said with false disappointment. "I'm sure you'd hate for me to run around unchaperoned."

That was an unveiled threat.

Perseus considered it for a moment. "I have a moment or two. I will show you around."

"I'd rather one of your lovely ladies showed me around," Anastase said as he looked over me, Danya and the quiet Angelica. I didn't like how he looked at her and put my hand on her arm, possessively.

"I'm sorry but we're very busy right now with our customers and need to get back to work. Perseus will take care of you," I said.

Giselle replied, "I'd love for him to take care of me."

Anastase patted her hand but spoke to me. "I see you cherish different kinds of company these days, my love."

He was referring to Angelica and I stood my ground, then Angelica spoke up.

"Yes, well, what we mean to each other is no concern of yours."

She placed her hand on mine as I glared at Anastase. Danya fumed as she fought the urge to pounce on Giselle. I glanced at her and shook my head. Danya saw it and stepped back behind me.

Anastase chuckled. "Be careful with your new pupil. I'd hate for her to misstep her boundaries. You never know what sort of creature may meet up with her on a dark night."

I reached my free hand out to stop Danya before she jumped forward and said, "At least some pupils can be taught boundaries. Some just never learn anything at all."

He roared with laughter and waved in front of himself for the tour to begin. I kept my hand on both women, just in case he turned around.

Perseus quickly moved them away from the door and toward the bar. I mentally told both Danya and Angelica to watch themselves as we went about our individual duties. Danya and I decided to canvass the bar to make sure Anastase and Giselle wouldn't make any crazy moves toward our customers. At one point, I saw Anastase deeply kiss Giselle in a dark corner on the second floor before they went back downstairs. I hid my jealousy and disgust.

About twenty minutes later, I mentally asked Danya if she saw our illustrious duo anywhere. She said she saw the back of them as they had headed to the front door. Just then there was a loud crash as a waitress dropped a whole tray of food by the bar. We both went to help her and were distracted doing so for a few minutes.

I then had an overwhelming feeling something bad had happened. I stood very still and concentrated. It was Angelica. She was leaning against an outside wall, away from the exit. I grabbed Danya, called to Perseus and quickly got to the side of the building where Angelica was crouched. Her breath was ragged and I smelled Anastase and Giselle in the air. They had compelled her to come outside and had drunk from her. This was another one of his threats against me, he was going to keep attacking my loved ones until I did as he wanted. This couldn't keep happening. How many people would be hurt because of me?

I helped her stand up and saw the bite wounds at her neck and on one wrist. She was very weak from the large amount they had taken from her. I kissed her on the forehead as I carefully picked her up. Danya watched out for me as I jumped up and onto the fire escape on the third floor. It led to the large window of Perseus' office. I broke the window lock and laid her gently on a leather couch by the fireplace.

Danya had followed me and I knew Perseus was coming up the inner stairs. I told him that she'd be okay but was weak; she'd need to rest for a couple of days. Danya mentally blamed herself for not watching the door better, but I told her that the fiend would've gotten to Angelica any way that he could have. Perseus patted Danya on the shoulder and held her hand as I decided to check the building again. I needed to make sure they were gone before I took Angelica home; I couldn't have them follow me.

Once all was clear, Danya and I took Angelica to her new home and placed her in the care of one of her neighbors. Angelica had been coherent enough to understand that she was to stay in bed the following day and not to answer the door for anyone. I told her to call me if anything strange happened. She'd been lucky that she hadn't been changed like Danya had been and she knew it.

Just as I was leaving, Angelica remembered something that Giselle had said during her attack. It was in regards to Jean Luc getting the dirt on Angelica and I, then laughing. I stopped and asked her to repeat it as best she could.

"That red haired bitch said that she was looking forward to seeing the dirt that Jean Luc was digging up on you," Angelica said with hatred.

I tried to make out what Giselle meant by that. Anastase and his crew already knew everything about me, so there wasn't anything to dig up.

Then it hit me.

Oh no. *Dig up.* Jean Luc was at my house and he was going to take the crates of dirt from my cellar.

I had to stop him, but knew I wasn't going to make it in time. I could only hope he wasn't going to find the small pouches I had hidden in my bedroom.

I concentrated on Perseus and told him what I thought was going on. He wanted to head to the house immediately, but couldn't just walk away from the bar at that moment, in case Anastase came back. I agreed and knew Danya could come with me. We took Perseus' sports car and headed home with the lights off and the pedal to the floor.

I pulled up to the house and saw that the door had been left open when Jean Luc had left. He wanted me to know that someone had been there. I smelled him in the air and I also caught Thomãs' scent. Danya had caught the scent as well and I had to tell her who it belonged to. She had hoped to never see that man again, because she'd kill him whether he had been compelled or not.

I ran down to the cellar as I sent Danya to check Perseus' bedroom. The crates had been removed and only one small pile of dirt had been left as the boxes had been carried out of the cellar door to the back alley. I met Danya half way and she shook her head. It was gone. I had enough that I could bag up from outside but that wouldn't be enough for both my brother and I. We could go to River Street and at least get some more of the bloodied dirt for Danya.

I told her what we'd have to do and I bagged up the remaining dirt from Cartagena. I hoped it was enough for us to get by on before we could take a trip back to our homeland. Danya would have to visit the scene of her own crime as well. I held her hand and flew us back to where it had happened for her. We both gasped at what we saw.

The ground had been covered in concrete, in a six-foot section. Someone had even drawn a happy face with Danya's initials. We were not amused; we'd have to bust it up in order to get to what was needed. But there were too many people around who'd certainly question two women busting up concrete with their bare hands.

Danya panicked since no dirt meant no restful sleep until it was recovered. This meant that energy and any special powers would decrease at an alarming rate. Danya was new and ran through blood faster than Perseus and I did.

I sent a message to Perseus informing him of what had happened. He decided to leave but would pick up Bambara on the way home. After mentally reaching out to Frank, he agreed to watch over the new staff on Saturday. Perseus would feed before he left town and again once he got home. We'd have to keep ourselves strong since we'd either have to get the crates back or go to Cartagena to get more.

Coming up with a plan, I told Danya that I'd cause a diversion a few hundred feet away so she'd have a few seconds to smash the concrete before people noticed her. Using my vampire speed, I whipped up the pavilion in a whirl so fast that leaves scattered and skirts rose. I smashed a light fixture and it crashed, causing just enough noise to muffle the concrete breaking. I ran further down the street while she grabbed her plastic bag full of dirt and we ran together back for the house.

We hid the bag in the house safe before we headed out to feed. We ended up at another cemetery where several ex-convicts were having a party, celebrating their release from jail for a teenager's murder. They had all gotten out on bond due to over crowding and had gone back to their old ways. We knew they were guilty and it would be fine if we killed them all. There was no remorse in any of them.

We began to feed and were on our second victim apiece when Danya caught a scent that floated on the air. Before I could stop her, she had dropped her prey and taken off. I concentrated on her and picked up the same scent. It was Jean Luc. I saw her chase after his laughing figure as he played with her in a swamp area not too far away.

I followed but was too late. By the time I'd gotten there he'd ambushed her and had slit her throat. He had run off laughing. I ran my tongue over her neck to heal her faster. I bit my wrist, fed her some of my blood and hoped she would heal enough to get out of there. I also hoped that the potion I had taken wouldn't hurt her, but I had to take the chance. Within moments, she'd gotten back on her feet. But she'd need more blood soon as a result of the injury. A quick read of her thoughts told me she was mad at herself for thinking she could take Jean Luc on, and realized that this was why we couldn't let her get her revenge just yet. She hadn't learned enough to beat these immortals and anger only made it worse. She'd have her day, I knew she would, but it'd have to wait a little longer.

I flew her back home just as Perseus drove up with Bambara. He had moved quickly after calling her to get here on time. Danya hung her head and slowly walked upstairs as Bambara came in with her bags. I sent Perseus up after Danya and Bambara shooed him away since she needed a moment alone with me. I gave her a quick summary of the events at hand and what had just happened to Danya. Bambara just shook her head; she knew the ways of the angry immortal and how it could consume them.

Perseus brought a resigned Danya back downstairs and we all sat down to discuss strategy. Perseus was furious over what had happened to Danya and how they were determined to come after us both. The more he spoke, the more worked up he became and eventually Perseus had to excuse himself for a moment to go outside and calm down. But after a few minutes of further discussion with Bambara, it hit me—I couldn't feel my brother's presence outside anymore. He hadn't walked out to get calm; he'd walked out to go after Jean Luc. He was trying to keep me out of his head, but his anger kept him from being focused. I had warned him not to do this, as Danya was proof of what they could do, but he saw himself as stronger and more controlled. I concentrated and saw a vision of him getting over-powered as pain blossomed in my head. The pain kept me from being able to see what had specifically happened to Perseus.

Bambara had seen my images, felt my pain, and nodded. We would keep him from getting killed. Thankfully, Justin was at home and distracted as he developed new photos. Bambara and I would leave Danya here, unaware of what her love had done, and run to the warehouse where I knew Perseus had gone.

"I see that look on your face. I may not be psychic but I can sense danger. Plus I know when my best friend is up to something," Danya said.

I looked over at her and knew she wanted to come with us, but I wasn't sure that she could handle this plan. Her anger at Jean Luc and Giselle plus her love for Perseus could be either bad or good. I didn't want her to fly off in anger again and we couldn't fight Anastase while we looked out for both of them, but it could also make her focused. I knew I couldn't stop her from following us, but I hoped she knew what she was doing.

"Are you sure about this? Your body just went through major changes and I'm not sure what you can handle. Don't do this to get even, do it to protect Perseus. If you go in there with anger, then you won't be focused enough to use your new powers."

Her glowing eyes looked back at mine and I knew that I couldn't change her mind.

"Yes, I'll go in there and do what I have to. Those people will not be allowed to walk away. I won't sit by while another person gets attacked. You either accept me as an ally or you don't, it's your choice."

She was a woman after my own heart. I reached out my hand and she took it.

"Welcome to the family, Danya. I've wanted you as my sister for years."

She shook my hand and I knew there'd be time for happiness later; we had to deal with this first.

We all headed to the front door of the warehouse, but I saw through Perseus' eyes as I made it over the threshold. He was facing Jean Luc and Giselle as he came through the door and they both advanced on him. He was so fast that I almost didn't see him. By the time they turned around, he was perched on an old metal desk near the exit door. Jean Luc laughed.

"We don't have the time to play, little Percy," Jean Luc said with a cocky grin.

Perseus tilted his chin forward. "We're immortal. We have all the time in the world."

"Ah, but that's not always true. You see, we left your little ladies with no time to worry. Didn't we?" He laughed again.

"Yes, it was quite a shame. You seem to have a knack for caring about fragile mortals," Giselle said sadly, but it was obvious she wasn't sad at all. This got to Perseus.

Then Giselle spoke to Jean Luc. "*Cherie*, I don't think little Percy knows the truth about Valentina. You see, Jean Luc was the one who attacked her in that dirty old alley. But she was the one who killed herself for what she'd become. That twist was just a bonus." She said it with mock ignorance.

I could feel his rage run through him. He had always wanted to know who had taken away his first love. And now he knew. This was going to get complicated. I whispered the current events to Bambara as the scene played in my mind. I felt the girls grab me.

Perseus charged Jean Luc as Giselle's cackling laughter followed them.

"I have wanted to kill her murderer for decades, and now I realize it was you. Why?" He asked as they stood facing each other. It was Jean Luc who answered.

"Well, I wanted your sis, but she wouldn't have anything to do with me. Then along comes your blushing bride to be. She was beautiful and intriguing, especially since she didn't know what she was about to marry. The problem was that the lady thought I was crazy and wanted no part of me. Some dames just need persuasion. Women back then weren't built to take the truth of stressful things and she passed right out. So, seeing as she couldn't complain, I had me sweet way with her. She felt so good, and then she woke up. She saw the fangs and went into hysterics. I tore out her lovely white throat to shut the lass up. Shame, really. She would have made quite an exquisite vampire if she hadn't burned herself alive for being one of us. *Tsk, Tsk.*"

That's when Perseus attacked. I could still hear their mocking laughter as he charged. Things happened quickly and I saw a dark man emerge from the back exit. Then Perseus was down. I could feel the blood being drained from him. Both Jean Luc and Giselle had him pinned down. Jean Luc sank his fangs down into the bone at Perseus' wrists while Giselle went for the vein at his neck. Perseus couldn't move. An invisible force held him as he was drained. I saw Giselle fling her head back from Perseus' neck, spit out a chunk of his flesh, and lick the blood from her lips. Jean Luc took a moment more before he did the same. I could feel Perseus' weakness as they moved away from his body. My vision faded as I felt his body being dragged away.

Chapter Fifteen

When my sight cleared, I looked at the girls and they saw the terror in my eyes.

"We have to save him. He'll die. Danya, use your sense of smell to seek him out and stay with us. And please don't be heroic. We have to stay together."

"Ok, let's see what this new body can do." She sighed and squared her shoulders. I felt her focus and she was strong.

With Bambara on my left and Danya on my right, I held their hands and we were off. Bambara had her own secrets of travel, but she used me for this particular trip. It took only a few minutes to reach the warehouse and we stopped two buildings over. We were downwind so we could group together before they became aware of us.

Bambara opened her robe just enough for me to see her ritual knife hidden there. She sent me an image of who the weapon was intended for. I only knew a few details about Olivier. I knew he was the father to her daughter Claudette and I knew that the relationship had ended when he'd gotten in too deep with black magic during the first two months of her pregnancy. She had banished him without even telling him of their child and had not looked back since. She knew he was back to make a stand, and if he defeated us, he could go after her daughter. She had spent too much effort in hiding Claudette to have him hurt them now. She would give her life to keep her daughter safe. The terror had to end. I understood her feelings and would do the same for any of my loved ones. We decided to use Danya as a decoy. They'd expect someone to show up, but she'd use her rage as a front and distract them as Bambara and I went for Anastase and Olivier. We had hoped Danya would be held with Perseus and could help him get out. It was risky, but we were out powered and out numbered.

Danya flew to the main door and waited for them to smell her, then walked into the open double doors. Through her eyes, I saw the look of surprise on Giselle's face and lust on Jean Luc's.

Neither had thought she would confront them. They mistakenly thought she was too weak.

But in reality, the change only intensified her strong backbone.

They both charged her and I saw her jump up into the rafters of the high metal ceiling. They chased each other back and forth as Bambara and I made our way closer to the small back exit. I felt pain as I saw Danya being grabbed by Giselle and slammed into the concrete floor. Jean Luc joined them and held Danya down as Giselle slammed Danya's head with several blows to the concrete. She started to bleed and was losing consciousness. Her attackers were giddy and distracted, just as planned.

Bambara and I ran into the room to grab them off of her. I flung them both off as Bambara ran to pick Danya up. Then in a flash, they were back at Danya's side and pushed Bambara ten feet away. I flew to Danya and saw a silver glint move quickly in an arc in front of her. Giselle screamed so loud that the metal building reverberated, clutched her hand to her bleeding face, and flung with all of her might at Danya. Danya was thrown up into the rafters on the other side of the warehouse and collapsed under some of the debris. I heard metal hit the ground and flew to retrieve what I knew was Bambara's ritual blade.

I grabbed Bambara and handed her blade back to her. Even thought she had her own power, she'd need it to defend herself. Amazingly, Giselle's wound wouldn't heal up. I suspected that it was the power of the blade that infected it. I'd have to make sure I didn't get cut by that same blade. Giselle, in a blood rage, flew up and broke off a piece of the rafter then drove it into Danya's stomach. Danya let out a cry as deafening as Giselle's. I had to get her out of this warehouse before they killed her.

The pain in my head increased to debilitating levels. It wasn't just the pain of my loved ones that I felt; it was more. I fought to focus my powers. This was the worst the pain had ever been. Then I felt Perseus stagger into the room as his wounds started to close up. He jumped onto Jean Luc's back and broke his thick neck. As I heard the break, I felt the vengeance as a sweet taste on my tongue.

Bambara knew what had caused me to be in such intense pain, her ex-lover had just walked in with my maker. She had warned him to stay away many years ago and had hidden her pregnancy away from him. She knew Claudette would be in danger if he found out about her. She immediately blocked the image of her daughter, away at college, and felt him look her way.

"Hello, my priestess," he mocked her with a low bow.

"You never should have come back. You *will* pay for this," Bambara said as she let the fury grow inside her.

Unlike these vampires, she was able to turn her fury into power, and tried to never get mad because of this very reason. Now, she would let it reign. One of them would not survive this night.

Olivier took up a stance in front of Anastase and we knew he'd protect Anastase at all cost. This would be the true battle. Bambara stood over me and started chanting. I saw Olivier cringe then start chanting as well. Bambara swayed as the dark magic hit her, but she focused while she chanted louder. Olivier was only marginally affected.

Anastase called out something; Olivier looked over at me. I immediately felt the pain intensify as it grew down to my stomach. I felt the power grip me with invisible hands. I felt myself being pulled toward Anastase, the last person I wanted to walk toward.

Bambara saw me move toward Anastase and Olivier so she charged toward Olivier with a pouch she had pulled from her neck. She flung the contents at Olivier before I was two feet away from him and she chanted again. The powder turned to an ochre smoke as it billowed into Olivier's lungs. He howled. At that moment I was able to stop myself from getting any closer. Anastase shot to me before I could gather my strength back. I was repulsed that his arms were around me but I wasn't able to move away from him.

I moaned, "No" as he looked down into my half open eyes.

"Yes. You belong to me and cannot stop me anymore." He stroked my face.

I looked over my shoulder to see Bambara fling herself at the smoking body of Olivier. Bambara vaulted onto Olivier's chest, placing her hands on each side of his dark face. He howled in pain as her chant gathered power. Then, in a flash, he clapped his hands above his head, with the sound of thunder. Bambara was thrown several feet from him. I saw a glint of metal as her body hit a stack of old pallets and then went limp against the broken wood. Blood started to pool around the splinters that had pierced her skin.

I saw Olivier come closer towards us, his ears streamed with dark blood. I felt ghostly ribbons wrap around my body and against Anastase's. He threw back his head in an animalistic moan and I knew he felt the same invisible ribbon.

I saw then that Olivier had something in his hand. When I looked closer, I saw it was a handmade doll; and it looked like me. He lifted it up before tying a black ribbon around it. The invisible ribbon around my body became taut. This new pain merged with the screaming pressure inside my skull. I screamed my pain and anger. I felt as if I was being suffocated to death by a supernatural enemy.

I felt Justin seep into my mind. I must've accidentally sent him images of where I was because he was already headed to this warehouse. He mistakenly thought he could save me. I was terrified that he would perish because of me and remembered my vision when I had first met him. This was when he would die. I was helpless to protect him as my link to him was snapped in half. He'd be here in minutes with no possible way to defend himself. I felt Perseus for a brief moment and knew that he had sensed Justin as well.

I tried to push at the barriers around my body and cried out as they became stronger against my struggling mind. Olivier's chanting was all I could hear as Anastase bent his lips toward mine. His cold marble lips took possession of my open ones. As soon as his lips caressed mine, the ribbons ignited. My cold flesh incinerated with voodoo power. I screamed as the pain came back in shattering waves. Anastase's lips moved from my screaming ones and glided over my chin, down to my vulnerable neck.

I heard Justin yell out as he barged into the warehouse and saw me in Anastase's embrace. Perseus yelled for Justin to get out, but he ignored him. Through his thoughts I knew he'd rather die than have Anastase possess me. Giselle left a scent of fear as she fled the warehouse. She was never one to throw herself into battle for any purpose other than her own.

Olivier was too focused on me to see Danya slip down the rafter and move to Bambara's side. She shook Bambara until Bambara regained consciousness then Bambara grabbed the metal object she had held moments ago. I knew that was Olivier's ceremonial knife she had somehow stolen from him. Bambara walked toward Olivier as Danya lit a match under the crushed pallets. It ignited quickly as she escaped toward the wall. Perseus and Justin moved toward each other, Perseus standing in front of Justin as Anastase's sharp teeth sunk into my neck.

I screamed once more as he fed, then went utterly numb. I felt myself hit the ground and knew my loved ones would come to help me. Anastase soon hit the floor next to me. Through my heavy lidded eyes I could see him grasp my hands. He cried out to me as he too was consumed in his own pain. What had made him collapse? Justin ran over and pulled me from Anastase's weakened grasp.

Olivier bellowed again as he hit the floor. Justin leaned over me, not seeing Anastase reach with his extended claws as they drove into Justin's neck, through the cord of his talisman. Anastase's body began to writhe against me as Justin fell backwards, trying to stop the blood flowing from his neck.

Danya flew by and dropped something in my hand before she backed up a few feet. The flames grew closer, as if they wanted to be free of the old building; I needed to do something before they engulfed us. The dry, old contents of the room passed the flames around too easily. I looked down to see Bambara's dagger in my weak palm. Anastase started to rouse and reached for me. I shrank toward Justin. Was he still breathing? Anastase got on his knees before he yanked me toward his unyielding body.

I hadn't regained enough strength to fight him, but I felt stronger with each passing moment. I shook out of his grasp and bent over Justin as he began to lose pressure on his hold of his oozing wound. His loss of blood had him fading away too quickly. Bambara came over, covered in the thick black substance that was Olivier's evil blood, and knelt over Justin as she applied pressure to his wound.

Just then, Anastase grabbed at me one last time. He never saw the dagger that was gripped in my trembling hand. It went deep into his ribcage, like a knife through butter. He tried to scream but no sound emerged; his mouth just gapped open. One hand traced the lines of my face as the other went toward his heart. I could hear his heartbeat slowing; it matched the one of my beloved, behind me. Two men were dying and both by my own actions.

Anastase tried to stand but fell to his knees by Justin. Sensing danger, Danya flew around and shoved Anastase backward. He landed in his burning desk chair and slumped there. The hungry flames licked his marble flesh. He made no move until he was completely caught in the flames, and then howled one last time before the flames ate him whole.

Perseus grabbed Danya out of reach of the burning chair and looked around as he noticed that we were completely surrounded with hissing flames. He screamed for me to get out and ran Danya out of there. I grabbed Justin in my arms and Bambara held on to my shoulder as I flew the three of us threw the untouched exit door and away from the inferno.

We landed on the edge of the wharf just as an explosion went off. It must've reached the cars that had been parked on the other side of the metal room. There was the smell of gas in the air as metal confetti fell around us. Thankfully we were all intact.

Except Justin.

I fell to the ground as his breathing slowed.

"Please, don't leave me." I stroked his forehead. "It can't be like this. We said we'd keep this from happening." I cried as his heartbeat began to slow down.

Perseus came to me and resumed unneeded pressure on Justin's neck. Bambara prayed in the background as Danya cried for my loss.

Justin looked at me through hazy eyes. "I will not leave you. In this life or any other."

The red tears streamed down my face as I whispered, "I have killed you."

"I'm not dead. You have the power to stop this." He focused on my eyes as I read the thread of his thoughts.

No. He wanted me to change him, here and now, so he wouldn't die. Could I do this? I'd never changed anyone before and had never wanted to know how.

Bambara stopped praying and put her hand on my shoulder.

"Child, you can do anything. Do not fear what you do not know. Fear is for the things you can change but choose not to. Do not let this fear turn into life's regret."

She was telling me to become a monster. She wanted me to kill someone I loved. I had vowed never to do this to anyone. Ever. And a four hundred year old promise is very hard to break.

I looked down into those beautiful dying eyes and knew I had precious little time left. He reached for my hand and drew it to his heart. He was slick with sweat and blood. He wanted to be done with his agony.

Perseus called to me. "Andromeda, don't make the same mistakes I did. He knows what he wants and he accepted us for what we are. You're not damning him because the same one who damned both of us did that for you. It's not your fault that he's dying, but it'll be your fault if you let him go. Trust in yourself and trust in your love for this man."

I couldn't believe Perseus had said that. Danya walked over and sat behind Perseus as he tried to stop the last of Justin's life from seeping away. She looked at me and nodded. I knew the price she had paid and yet she didn't regret it. She was glad to have Perseus' love and would never look back. She was one of us and accepted it all. I needed to be brave like her.

"Justin, are you sure this is what you want? There's no going back once I've done this. You'll be a creature like me for eternity." I begged him to be reasonable but I didn't want him to go. My inner demon wanted him with me forever. Was that so bad?

Justin coughed up some of his life force and tried to speak but couldn't get the words out. He squeezed my hand and slid it to replace the one at his neck.

I heard him in my head, "Please, don't let me go."

His eyes drifted shut.

"*No!*" I screamed and threw everyone off of me.

I saw a tiny trickle of blood pool in his wound. I decided to embrace my power. I focused on that red nectar and let go of my inhibitions as I dug my teeth into that open wound. Justin gasped as I drank the last of his life away, and then flung my head back with a roar of rage. I would have to embrace the creature that I had sworn never to become. Justin went completely limp.

I heard Bambara whisper, "Hurry, child".

I bit into my wrist so hard that the bone cracked. I hung that wrist over the wound in Justin's neck and prayed that I would be forgiven for this selfishness. But I had committed to this and couldn't stop now. I squeezed until I felt lightheaded, and then placed that wrist in the wound so it would absorb everything I could give him. I waited there, like that, for what seemed an eternity. Nothing happened. Perseus held Danya as she sobbed. I foolishly tried to shake Justin awake. What had I done wrong? There was no heartbeat in my soul mate.

I heard the sirens and knew we had to get out of there quickly. I wasn't going to leave Justin behind so I gathered him to me as Danya and Perseus flew Bambara out of there. I held Justin and thought of my home. I was at the steps before I knew what happened and took my soul mate upstairs to my room. I walked past my three battle-worn loved ones, saying nothing as I laid Justin on my bed.

I didn't care if any blood got on my expensive sheets. I didn't care that they wanted me to let go of him. I told them all to go away as I climbed in bed with him. I was weary and weak from the traumatic night. I still hadn't been able to grasp all of the events that had happened. Life could wait. I cried for the battle I had fought, for the lives that had been damaged, for feeding the demon within, for being too late and for losing the man I'd been waiting for my whole immortal life.

* * * *

I stayed in my sweet oblivion for two days. I drank only from a glass when I was forced to, then promptly fell back into a depression driven slumber. My eyes came open as the fingers of the sun disappeared from the sky on that second day. I felt different. The events had changed me. I could no longer read others random thought patterns, as I had under the potion's influence. I was thirsty with a normal need to feed, but I couldn't bring myself to move off of the bed.

There was someone beside me. I looked over to see the face of my beloved, Justin, and the images of his death hit me. I began to cry but nothing came from my dry body. I leaned over to kiss his cold lips as my chest heaved with loss and pain. The lips pressed back. My God, he was kissing me. Was I insane? Had I lapsed into a vampiric coma? I didn't care. I kissed him right back. Then his eyes opened. I looked into the sparkling depths. He was alive and smiling at me. I screamed for joy as he quickly rolled on top of me and kissed the tears from my face.

The others burst into the room and saw us kissing each other as we laughed. Bambara clutched her heart and said a prayer of thanks. Danya and Perseus smiled as they reached for each other's hands. Justin had survived and he was a vampire like us. Everyone was still alive. I hadn't lost anyone except my pirate stalker.

Later that day, as Bambara and I sat down and watched the sun rise that day, we recreated the events through our joined powers.

We realized that Olivier had made a voodoo doll with personal items that had been taken from me. He had been trying to perform a binding spell on me so that I would be tied to Anastase for eternity. The amount of potion in me had helped to keep Olivier's spells at bay but had also poisoned Anastase. Bambara had stabbed Olivier with his own knife and the black on her had been his once powerful blood.

Bambara was free of her black magic lover. He could no longer bring fear into her life. This meant that she could finally put an end to Claudette being hidden away from her world. She could bring her daughter home.

Justin had not been too far gone to be changed, as we had thought, but we were both so depleted that the change had taken longer to complete. Justin had no remorse about being changed, and was only thankful he had a second life to live, with me. He moved in with me and had turned the apartment in the basement into his dark room for his film processing. He was still going ahead with his life as a photographer and decided that night photography would be his specialty.

Danya had moved permanently into the suite with Perseus, completing our family. My crates were found intact a little ways outside the warehouse that had burned down. Perseus and Bambara had gone the day after to look for Anastase's remains, but had found nothing; the chair had burned down to the metal. There should've been part of a corpse or at least his ashes, but there was nothing. There was no proof of his existence there and we'd have to live with that as long as we lived.

In days to come, I dreamed several pieces of a scene that I prayed was not true. In my dreams I saw a figure that had come in when the others had flown away from the flaming building. The figure had red hair and carried a charred burden away before sliding it into a rowboat. The red head was not conscious of the burnt doll in the remains of the hand she cradled close to her damned heart. There was no knowing what would become of that tortured bundle, for now.

The End

About the Author

I'm Georgia born, with Alabama roots, so I'm practically related to myself. I'm a mom, grandmother and a part time student who's sometimes seen in pirate wench or vampire gear. But, no matter how many personas I have, I'm eternally a writer.

I started writing my first manuscript at seventeen and it'll be my second book published, *Just to be Left Alone*. I typically write paranormal, but there will be a few other genres seeping out of my imaginative mental ramblings. I'm a third place winner in the Ozark Romance Writers Weta Awards for the Paranormal Division in 2011 plus a member with Romance Writers of America and Georgia Romance Writers. I currently have fifteen books plotted out and only need to wrangle time to get all of the voices out. My Savage Series will make up ten of those manuscripts, maybe more.

I live and breathe creativity. It doesn't matter if it's making the fully boned lacing corsets that I wear or if it's coming up with wicked one liners, in my sassy southern voice, for my fictional friends. I'm a firm believer in laughter being the best medicine, so I always carry a double dose with me.

)))Corset Hugs(((
Ginny Lynn
Wench Writer

Secret Cravings Publishing
www.secretcravingspublishing.com

Made in the USA
Charleston, SC
08 July 2013